ROCKSTAR *Regret*

LOVERS KNOT SERIES

MORGANA BEVAN

ABOUT THIS BOOK

Nick Davies was my best friend, my partner-in-crime. But that was before everything fell apart

Before our best friend's death shattered the world we shared. Before Nick left without looking back.

Now he's back. Except he's not just Nick anymore. Now he's *Nick Davies*, the tattooed, untouchable drummer for Lovers Knot, with a million-dollar smile, and an air of untouchable charm.

But none of that erases the boy who broke my heart — or the tension that sparks every time our eyes meet.

Thanks to a meddling matchmaker, we're trapped together in a farmhouse, surrounded by memories of our dead best friend while the village floods. He says he wants to fix things, but some things can't be fixed. And I'm not sure I'm ready to face what's been left unsaid for so long.

Rockstar Regret is a steamy, forced-proximity, second-chance romance about a small-town cheesemaker and the rock star who shattered her heart.

For readers who love meddling matchmakers, rising tensions, and the kind of storms that make running from the truth impossible

FOREWORD

1 - exile (feat. Bon Iver) - Taylor Swift

2 - Ghost Town - Benson Boone

3 - Remember That Night? - Sara Keys

4 - Shake It Out – Florence + The Machine

5 - Don't Light the Match - The Maine

6 - Caution - The Killers

7 - In My Veins (feat. Erin McCarley) by Andrew Belle

8 - Heaven in Hiding - Halsey

9 - Bleeding Out - Imagine Dragons

10 - Take on the World - You Me At Six

11 - Missing Place - Vance Joy

12 - This Love - Taylor Swift

If you'd like to listen to the playlist, it's on my Spotify profile here.

CHAPTER ONE

CERYS

*M*einir Williams was like a well-aged Caerphilly — sharp, a bit crumbly, and impossible to ignore. If I could box her up and ship her off to a fancy London cheese shop, I would.

No, really, I would...

Oh, who am I kidding? She owned the land my cheeses called home, and worse, she was my late boyfriend's mother.

But bloody hell, some days she made me want to tear my hair out and run screaming into the hills of the Brecon Beacons. And today? She'd outdone herself. I swear, that woman could try the patience of a saint — or a stubborn Welsh cheesemaker, which might be the tougher test.

The meddling pain in my ass had outdone herself today. I never thought she'd manage to strike *getting me to socialise outside the farmers' market* off the list, but she'd done it. Probably been plotting this longer than it takes to age a decent Cheddar, the crafty old goat.

I just wanted to do my job, get the next batch of Snowdonia Blue into the ageing room, pack some orders, and maybe clock out before the sunset for the first time in a bloody year.

But no, Meins hadn't agreed with those plans and had twisted my arm into lunch with that knowing look of hers. The one that made me feel like a naughty schoolgirl caught sneaking extra bara brith.

Had she spilled the beans on who she'd invited to lunch, I might have put up more of a fight.

Might have rubbed my fingers raw testing cheese textures to avoid it. Might have mysteriously developed a case of cheese cave fever. Anything to avoid... this.

But I hadn't, and now I stood in her old farmhouse kitchen, staring at the one man who could still make my heart do a jig worthy of the Eisteddfod with just a look.

Nick bloody Lewis.

I'd rather face a cranky ram than deal with this. At least the ram would be honest about wanting to knock me on my ass.

Nick stared back at me — or more at the spot to the right of my shoulder — appearing just as shocked as I felt, his blue eyes wide and darting between me and Meinir. The kitchen suddenly felt as stuffy as my ageing room in midsummer.

Christ, is the room shrinking?

"Cerys," he said, his deliciously gruff voice curling around my name exactly as it had in school. Only then I'd been his best friend, doing everything I could to pretend that he couldn't make me shiver with just a word.

Now? Now I was doing everything I could not to show how much it still affected me. Stupid, traitorous body.

His gaze skittered around the kitchen, bouncing from Meins to the kettle boiling on the stove and back. "I... didn't know you'd be here."

"That makes two of us," I said, my voice sharper than a well-honed cheese knife. I turned to the mischievous meddler, who was busying herself with the kettle, a suspiciously innocent expression on her face. "Meins, a word?"

But before I could drag her into the pantry for a proper Welsh telling-off, Nick cleared his throat. "Look, I should go. This was obviously a mistake—"

"Oh no, Nicky," Meinir said, her voice soft but with that edge I knew all too well. The one that could guilt a saint into eating another slice of cake. "You've only just got back from tour. Surely you can spare me an hour for lunch? I've made your favourite shepherd's pie and there's bara brith for dessert. Please stay. It's been ages since we've all sat down together. Gareth would want that, don't you think?"

Low blow, Meins.

I watched his resolve crumble. Though really, no one would be surprised. The woman was more tenacious than a choir director at the Eisteddfod.

He sighed, running a hand through his hair. "Right, of course. Sorry."

Before I could make my own escape — maybe I could fake a cheese emergency? Runaway Camembert? — she turned to me, her eyes twinkling like she'd just won Star Baker on The Great British Bake Off. "And you, Cerys fach. That cheese of yours can wait an hour. It won't kill you to take a break and eat your lunch sitting down for once."

I opened my mouth to argue, but Meins was already pushing us both towards the table. This was going to be a long, awkward lunch. And if I survived it without lobbing a wheel of cheese at someone's head, it'd be a miracle.

Preferably a nice, heavy wheel of Caerphilly.

At Nick's stupidly handsome face.

I glared at the placemat. "I'd rather be elbow-deep in curds and whey right now."

Nick snorted. "Some things never change, do they, Evans?"

I shot him a look that could curdle

milk. "And some people never learn when to keep their mouths shut, do they, Nicky?"

His jaw clenched, a muscle ticking in his cheek. His eyes, those impossibly blue eyes that used to make my teenage heart flutter, darkened. "Right. Because you're the expert on knowing when to stop talking."

I bristled, my fingers itching for that wheel of cheese. Why hadn't I thought to bring one in from my workshop? But before I could unleash a retort that would make a sailor blush, Meinir swooped in, her voice saccharine sweet.

"Now, now, you two. Let's not bicker. The pie is ready, and I've made a pot of tea. Shall we sit?"

I glanced at Nick, catching his eye for a brief moment. The silent communication we'd perfected years ago hadn't faded, it seemed. His slight eye roll matched my barely concealed sigh. We were both trapped in Meinir's web of good intentions and nostalgia.

"Fine," I muttered, dropping into a chair at the worn wooden table. Might as well get this over with.

If I ate fast enough, I could escape before Meins tried to make us sing Kumbaya or something equally horrifying.

Nick pulled out his own seat, the basic, simple action brushing déjà vu against my mind. How many times had we sat at this very table with Gareth, laughing and planning our futures back when the future seemed limitless and unbreakable? Back when we were young and stupid enough to believe that nothing could tear us apart.

God, we were idiots.

Meinir busied herself, setting out mismatched china cups and plates,, the cheerful clatter at odds with the tension humming between Nick and me. The rich, spicy scent of freshly baked bara brith filled the air, a comforting aroma that usually made me feel at home. Today, it just made my stomach churn.

Funny how even the most comforting things can turn sour when mixed with regret and resentment.

Outside, the December rain continued its relentless assault, pattering against the windows and streaming down the glass in fat rivulets. The gloomy Welsh winter had settled in with a vengeance, turning the world beyond the farmhouse into a grey, sodden mess. I suppressed a shiver, grateful for the warmth of the kitchen, even if the company left something to be desired.

"I hope you're both hungry," Meinir said, setting a steaming casserole dish in the centre of the table. "Nothing beats a good shepherd's pie on a day like this."

I had to admit, it did look delicious. Golden-brown mashed potatoes crusted the top, hiding the lamb and vegetable filling beneath.

On any other day, I'd be salivating. To-day, I wasn't sure I could stomach a bite.

"It looks great, Meins," Nick said, his voice warm. "Just like I remember."

I couldn't help but roll my eyes. "Careful there, rock star. Wouldn't want to ruin your fancy tour diet with home cooking."

"Don't be stupid. You know I've always loved Meins's cooking."

"Sure you have. That's why she barely sees you."

Nick shrugged, attempting a noncha-lant smile that didn't reach his eyes. "The band's been busy. Big tours, new music… you know how it is. I visit when I can."

"So you say." I'd never seen him on any of those visits. In the first few years after Gareth's death, he'd gone out of his way to make them as last minute as possible so Meins couldn't invite me. "I remember a time when you cleared your calendar for us." But that was before. I crossed my arms, trying to ignore the pang in my chest.

"It's hard for young artists," Meinir said, buying his empty excuses yet again. "I understand, and I appreciate every moment you gift me."

Nick nodded, but I continued to glare at him. He'd done everything he could to avoid us after Gareth's death. The kitchen fell silent, save for the soft tick of the ancient clock on the wall and the persistent drum of rain against the windows.

Meinir began serving generous portions onto our plates and despite my churning emotions, my stomach gave an involuntary growl.

Traitor.

As we ate, I couldn't tear my eyes away

from him, couldn't stop myself from taking in all the changes eight years had wrought. He was still unfairly attractive, damn him. His dark hair was longer now, artfully tousled in that way that probably took ages to perfect but was meant to look effortless. A day's worth of stubble shadowed his jaw, and I could see the edge of a tattoo peeking out from under the collar of his shirt.

He looked... different.

Older, of course, but there was something else. A weariness in the set of his shoulders, a tightness around his eyes that spoke of more than just jet lag.

For a moment, a flicker of concern jolted to life inside of me. Then I remembered the last time I'd seen him, at the hospital while the doctor delivered the news that Gareth had passed. The way he'd avoided my gaze, muttered some platitude about being sorry, and disappeared. The concern shrivelled, replaced by the familiar burn of resentment. Fool me once, shame on you. Fool me twice... Well, I wasn't about to let that happen.

"So, Nicky," Meinir said, breaking the

tense silence. "Tell me all about your tour. America, wasn't it?"

Nick shifted in his seat, clearly uncomfortable. Good. Let him squirm. Let him feel a fraction of the discomfort I've been living with for years.

"Yeah, we've been supporting The Brightside on their US tour. It's been... intense."

I couldn't help but snort. "Intense? What, the groupies too demanding?"

His eyes snapped to mine, a flash of hurt quickly masked by annoyance. "It's not like that. You know I'm not—"

I cut him off, my voice sharp enough to slice one of my prize-winning cheddars. "I don't know anything about you anymore, Nick. Eight years is a long time."

His face fell, and for a second, I glimpsed the boy I used to know — vulnerable and a bit lost. But then his jaw set, and he was back to being the stranger who'd walked into Meinir's kitchen. The boy I knew was gone, replaced by this... this rock star who couldn't be bothered to remember where he came from.

"That's not fair," he said, his voice low. "I've tried—"

"Tried what?" I shook my head. "To set a world record for avoiding your hometown?"

Meinir cleared her throat. "Now, now, let's not—"

"It's okay, Meins," Nick said, his eyes locked on mine. "Cerys has something to say. Let's hear it."

The challenge in his voice made my blood boil. Who did he think he was, waltzing back in here like nothing had changed?

"Oh, you want to hear it? Fine. How about we start with how you vanished after Gareth's funeral? Or how about the fact that you couldn't even be bothered to call in on his birthday last year?"

Nick flinched. "I was on tour. We had a gig—"

"Right, because heaven forbid you miss a show to remember your best friend." The words tasted bitter on my tongue, but I couldn't stop them. Years of pent-up anger and hurt were bubbling to the surface like an overflowing cheese vat.

This is why I'd avoided him *for eight years.*

"That's enough," Meinir said, her tone stern. "Both of you. This isn't why I invited you."

I turned my glare on her. "And why did you drag me out of my cheese room for this? To reminisce about the good old days? News flash: they're gone. Just like Gareth."

The moment the words left my mouth, I regretted them. Her face crumpled, and even Nick looked horrified. Shame washed over me, hot and suffocating. My throat closed up, choking on words I wished I could take back. Why had I said that? I never brought Gareth up to Meins. It was an unspoken rule, a line I'd never crossed.

Until now.

"I'm sorry," I managed to croak out. "That was... I shouldn't have said that."

Meinir took a deep breath, composing herself. "It's alright, cariad. I know you're hurting. We all are."

Nick pushed his food around his plate. "I should—"

"No," she snapped, surprising us both. "You're staying. Both of you. We're going to finish this meal, and we're going to talk. Like adults."

I opened my mouth to protest, but she gave me a look that would make a dragon think twice. I shut it again, feeling like a scolded child. Which, to be fair, was pretty much how I was acting.

"I've been meaning to give you something," Meins said before the silence could stretch any further.

She walked over to the old oak sideboard. Opening a cupboard, she pulled out a worn cardboard box and set it deliberately at the end of the table where neither of us could escape it. My stomach plummeted.

"It's Gareth's things. Bits and pieces I thought you both might want."

I stared at the box, my throat going dry. "Meins, I don't think—"

"No," Nick said, his voice strained. "I can't go through that."

Her expression hardened. "You've avoided this long enough. Both of you. It's time to face the past instead of running from it."

"I'm not running," I snapped, though

the quiver in my voice betrayed me. "I just don't see the point."

"If you won't take the time to go through them, I'm throwing them out."

"You wouldn't," I whispered, shocked. Gareth was her son. She kept everything of his, from childhood drawings to his old rugby boots. His room was like a freaking shrine.

"Try me." She lifted her chin defiantly. "I've held on to this for eight years. It's time to let go."

Nick swallowed hard, his eyes fixed on the box. "Meinir, please. Not today."

"Yes, today," she said, her tone hard. "You two need to confront this, together."

A heavy silence settled over the kitchen, broken only by the relentless rain hammering against the windows. It felt like the walls were closing in on me, the air thick with unspoken words and suppressed emotions.

"Fine," I finally muttered, crossing my arms over my chest. "But don't expect miracles."

Nick glanced at me, his expression a

mix of relief and resignation. "Alright. We'll get it over with."

Meins nodded, a small, satisfied smile tugging at her lips. "Thank you. Both of you." She took her seat again. "Now," she said, her voice softening. "Did you get to see much of America, Nicky?"

He hesitated, glancing at me before answering. "Not really. It was mostly hotels and venues. We did get a couple of days off here and there." His lips curved into a little smirk, a look he got when he was about to wind me up.

My eyes narrowed on the little shit, bracing myself for whatever crap was about to come out of his mouth.

"I finally got to see Boston, though."

Envy instantly speared through me, sharp and hot as a knife through soft cheese. Just like he knew it would.

Boston. He'd gone without me.

I felt like I'd been sucker-punched. It wasn't fair.

"What was it like?" The words slipped out before I could stop them.

Nick's eyes lit up. "It was great. We had a whole day off, so I did the full tourist thing. Walked the Freedom Trail, saw Fenway Park. But the best part? We passed by the Boston Police Headquarters — you know, the one from Rizzoli & Isles? And I swear I saw a café that looked just like The Dirty Robber."

"Did you get to go inside?" I asked, aiming for casual and missing by a mile. The words came out softer than I intended, betraying my interest. Betraying the part of me that still cared, that still wanted to share this with him.

"Yeah, actually." Nick's grin widened, and I could see the excitement dancing in his eyes. "I convinced the guys to grab a drink there. It wasn't exactly like in the show, but man, it felt surreal."

The image hit me like a ton of bricks. Nick, sitting in the bar we'd dreamed about, living out our shared fantasy without me. It shouldn't hurt this much, not after all this time. But it did. It felt like he'd taken a piece of our past, of us, and made it his alone.

"That's… that's great," I managed, the words tasting like ashes in my mouth. "I'm glad you got to see it." The lie sat heavy on my tongue, but what else could I say? That I was jealous? That it should have been me there with him? That he had no right to our dreams anymore?

"I took some photos," Nick said, his voice softening. "If you want to see them later, I mean."

Later. As if we'd be hanging out after this forced lunch. As if we were friends again, sharing stories and swapping photos like old times. As if the last eight years hadn't happened, hadn't changed us both.

I stabbed at a piece of lamb, focusing on my food to hide the conflicting emotions on my face.

Don't fall for it, Cerys.

He'll be gone again before you can say 'cheese curd.' This isn't the start of something new. It's just a reminder of everything you've lost.

Meinir leaned forward, her eyes shining with pride. "Did you get to try any of the local food?"

While Nick gushed over Boston cream pies and clam chowder, I found myself torn between wanting to hear every detail and wanting to plug my ears. Each word was a reminder of what I'd missed out on, of the life he'd lived while I'd stayed behind, tethered to this place.

Part of me wanted to lash out, to hurt him like his words were hurting me. But another part, a part I thought I'd buried years ago, wanted to ask if he'd thought of me while he was there. If he'd wished, even for a moment, that I was there with him.

Instead, I sat there, silent, letting his words wash over me like the rain outside. And all the while, that traitorous heart of mine kept beating, kept hoping, kept wondering what it would be like if things had been different.

"... and the gig tonight is huge," Nick said, pulling me back to the present. "If all goes well, we could be signed by tomorrow morning."

"Oh, cariad, that's wonderful!" Meinir clapped her hands together, beaming like she'd just won first prize at the county show. "I always knew you'd make it big. Didn't I tell you, Cerys? Our Nicky, a real rock star."

I forced a smile, ignoring the twinge in my chest. "Yeah, great."

He met my gaze, and for a moment, I saw a flicker of... something. Uncertainty? Guilt? Before I could decipher it, he looked away, focusing on Meins again. Coward.

"It's not a done deal yet," he said, running a hand through his hair. "But the label seems interested. They're sending some execs to the show tonight."

"You'll blow them away, I'm sure," she said, reaching out to pat his hand. "You always had the talent."

I couldn't help but roll my eyes. *Christ, why don't you just build him a shrine in the living room, Meins?*

"I'm sure the fancy hair and tattoos don't hurt either."

His jaw clenched. "It's not about the image. It's about the music. Always has been."

"Right," I scoffed, unable to keep the bitterness from my voice. "Because nothing says 'it's all about the music' like playing support for the pop band flavour of the month."

"One, The Brightside aren't a pop band," Nick said, his voice tight. "Two, they're a multi-award winning, international rock sensation who helped Marable put Wales on the music map. Third, they're incredibly talented musicians and they've given us more amazing opportunities than we deserved."

Bitterness burned inside of me and I despised the person it turned me into around Nick. This angry, spiteful version of myself that I barely recognised. But I also didn't want to stop it. It was easier to be angry than to admit how much his absence still hurt.

"And here I thought you might have had the chance to write something original instead of riding their coattails," I said, my fork stabbing through a piece of meat with unnecessary force. The screech of metal on china made me wince, but I didn't back down.

A muscle ticked in Nick's jaw. "You know what? Sometimes support slots are just the beginning. It's how you build your career."

"Now, now, children," Meins said before I could come up with a cutting retort. "Let's not turn this into a battle." She narrowed her eyes on me, silently telling me to get my shit together. If only I could. Then she turned her focus back to him. "Tell me about your new music."

His brow furrowed, and he hesitated, searching my eyes. "We're working on our next album. It's more... personal." The vulnerability in his voice caught me off guard. "Like we finally decided to stop hiding behind the noise and actually write about things that matter."

"Really?" I feigned interest, but the anger simmered below. "What kind of things? Girlfriends and parties?"

He shot me a look filled with disdain, sharpening that undercurrent of connection we so desperately tried to ignore. "No. I write about life, Cerys. About loss. Regret."

It must be nice to think that the world could be reduced to mere music notes and catchy lyrics for him. Meanwhile, I lived here, surrounded by the memories of what we'd had and what we'd lost. The idea that Nick could wrap his loss in a melody and suddenly feel better felt like a sick joke.

Before I could fire back, Meinir stood

up abruptly. "Oh! Oh dear, I've just re-membered. I have an appointment in town. I have to go."

I narrowed my eyes, suspicion creeping in. "An appointment? Now?"

Pull the other one, Meins. It's got bells on.

She was already gathering her things, moving with a speed that belied her years. "Yes, yes. Very important. Can't miss it. You two finish your lunch, alright?"

"Meins, wait—" Nick started, but she was already at the door.

"Sorry, cariad. We'll catch up again. Must dash. Enjoy your lunch!"

CHAPTER TWO

NICK

I hadn't seen it coming. Hell, I hadn't even suspected it.

The manipulative genius of Meinir had completely blindsided me. The door slammed shut behind her, the sound echoing through the old farmhouse. My heart skipped a beat, and not in the good way. Being alone with Cerys Evans? Terrifying didn't begin to cover it.

The woman had made it her mission to remind me of every mistake I'd ever made. Her glares could freeze hell over, I swear.

I stared at her, trying to reconcile the

woman before me with the girl I'd known. Her hair was longer, pulled back in a practical braid, but a few wisps had escaped to frame her face. She'd always been beautiful, but there was a sharpness to her features now, a hardness in her eyes that hadn't been there before. Was that my fault too?

I'd come back to the farm to see Meinir, like I always did when I passed through town. It had become a tradition, something I felt I owed her after Gareth's death. A small penance, perhaps, for not being there when it mattered most.

I hadn't expected Cerys. And if I'd known she was going to be here, I probably would've run the other way.

Coward.

The silence stretched between us, thick and suffocating. My fingers itched to grab my drumsticks, to fill the quiet with a rhythm, any rhythm. Instead, I shoved my hands into my pockets to keep from fidgeting.

Part of me wanted to fill it with words, explanations, apologies — anything. But what could I say that I hadn't tried to say a hundred times before? Every rehearsed line felt hollow now.

I shifted in my seat at the old wooden table, wishing I was anywhere but here — back on stage, mid-set, drumsticks whirling in my hands as I got lost in the beat.

"So..." I said, trailing off awkwardly.

"So," Cerys echoed, suddenly very interested in the pattern on her plate.

"Remind me never to play poker with that woman." I forced a chuckle that sounded hollow even to my own ears.

She grunted, but continued to study her plate like it held the secrets of the universe.

"Did you have any idea she was planning this little ambush?"

She turned her head just enough to glance at me, her green eyes sharp. "If I had, do you think I'd be here?"

Fair point.

She let out a derisive snort. "She's meddling where she's not wanted."

I bit back a sigh. Talking to Cerys these days was like navigating a minefield — one wrong step and everything blew up in my face.

"Look, I didn't come here to cause trouble. I just wanted to see Meinir before heading back on tour."

"Well, you've seen her," she said, her tone icy. "No one's stopping you from leaving."

Ouch. Harsh, but true. Yet even with that knowledge, I didn't move from my seat.

"Probably not wise for me to drive the country lanes when it's bucketing it down."

She shrugged, folding the tea towel with precise movements. "You're a big boy. I'm sure a bit of rain won't melt you."

Her words stung more than they should have. I clenched my jaw, swallowing the retort that threatened to spill out.

There was no point in arguing. Not with her. Not after all these years.

I cleared my throat, desperate to break the suffocating silence. "So... how's the cheese business?"

Cerys stiffened in her chair, her movements slow and deliberate as she picked up her cup. She arched an eyebrow, finally glancing up at me. "It's fine."

"Just fine?" I offered a tentative smile.

"Meins mentioned you've been winning awards."

Her expression remained guarded. "She exaggerates."

"Still, it's impressive. You always had a knack for it."

She crossed her arms, eyes narrowing slightly. "You wouldn't know. You haven't been around."

There it was — the dagger slipped between the ribs. I resisted the urge to rub my chest where the phantom pain settled. I'd had years of practice hiding my emotions from the press, from fans, from myself.

"Fair enough, but I always knew you had it in you."

She snorted, a sound caught between derision and amusement. "Right. Because you've been so involved in my life lately."

I winced internally but didn't let it show. The urge to flee warred with the need to make things right, somehow. But how do you mend eight years of silence and blame?

"Look, I know I haven't been around much, but—"

"Save it," she cut me off, pushing back from the table. The legs of her chair scraped against the stone floor, the sound grating on my nerves. "I don't need your half-assed apologies or your pity. I'm doing just fine without you."

She stood, gathering the plates with sharp, efficient movements. The clink of china seemed unnaturally loud in the tense quiet. Her hands trembled ever so slightly. Or maybe that was just my wishful thinking.

"Here, let me help." I reached for a dish.

Our hands brushed, and we both jerked back as if burned. For a split second, I was seventeen again, sneaking glances at Cerys across the classroom, my heart racing every time she smiled. But those stolen looks were always tinged with guilt. She was Gareth's girl, utterly off-limits. I'd buried those feelings deep, channelling them into my music.

Now, her eyes held no warmth, just a weary resignation that cut deeper than any glare.

"I've got it," she said, her voice

clipped. "You'd probably just break something anyway."

I bit back a sigh and slumped back into my chair. This was going nowhere fast.

I should just leave.

My eyes followed Cerys around as she efficiently cleaned up the kitchen. The half-eaten shepherd's pie sat in front of me.

Part of me wanted to shovel it down, fulfilling my promise to Meins so I could bolt. But another part, the part I'd been trying to silence for years, knew I owed Cerys more than that. Still, I found myself picking up my fork, pushing the food around my plate as I searched for something, anything, to say.

My legs jiggled under the table — an old habit I couldn't get a handle on. The tension humming between us was thick enough to drown in, but I wasn't about to run yet. Meinir could storm in any second with dessert, tell us to play nice, and maybe this would all blow over — or, at the very least, I could retreat back to the life waiting for me outside her farmhouse door.

"And, um, how's your dad?" I asked,

grasping for any thread of conversation. "Is he giving you a hard time for changing things up in the business?"

The plate in Cerys's hand clattered into the sink. There was a moment of silence that seemed to stretch like a cat waking from a nap — slow, deliberate, more dangerous than it looked.

She turned to face me, her expression a mix of disbelief and bitter amusement. She met my eyes, her gaze hard. "My father passed away last year, Nick. Another funeral you missed."

My heart sank to somewhere around the floor. "Shit, I... I had no idea. I'm..."

"Sorry?" she finished for me, the fire in her eyes sparking brighter.

A flash of lightning outside punctuated her words, briefly illuminating the kitchen in harsh white light.

"Don't bother. Your apologies don't mean much." Her tone turned bitter. "I don't know why I was stupid enough to hope you might show up. You couldn't even do that for Gareth."

The name — his name — hung heavy

between us, cutting through the thin veil of civility we'd been clinging to. And just like that, I knew we were headed straight into the thick of it, and there was no avoiding it now.

A familiar tightness gripped my chest, the old guilt resurfacing with a vengeance. I didn't know how to respond.

For years, I'd rehearsed all the things I could say if I saw her again, something that could explain why I stayed away without sounding like the complete coward I was. But now, staring into her fire-spitting eyes? All those words tangled up in my throat.

When I didn't respond, she sighed and wiped her hands on a tea towel, the motion brisk.

"If you're not going to leave, we should get that over with." She gestured to the cardboard box I'd diligently tried to ignore.

"You mean... now?"

"Yes, now." She arched a brow, a hint of impatience flashing in her eyes. "Unless you'd prefer to drag this out even longer. Frankly, the sooner we do this, the sooner we can both get back to our lives and never have to see each other again."

Ouch. Not that I didn't deserve it. Still, hearing her say it so bluntly sent a sharp pang through my chest.

"Fine," I muttered, pushing myself up from the table. "Let's get it over with."

"Fine." Her gaze fell to the worn cardboard and mine begrudgingly followed.

How could something so innocent looking contain so much potential for pain?

Cerys reached out, her fingers hovering over the dusty cardboard. Hesitation radiated from her and I couldn't blame her. We'd spent so much time in this house growing up, spent so many hours with Gareth, experienced so many firsts together. There would only be good memories inside that box, but even knowing that with absolute certainty, the thought of opening it, of exposing those happy times to life without him…it was the last thing I wanted to do.

I couldn't believe Meins would ever throw Gareth's things out, but that didn't mean I was willing to risk it.

Which left one option.

Swallow the lump in my throat and get my shit together.

Finally, Cerys released the haphazard criss-cross holding it shut. We each stared at it again. I wouldn't be surprised if we held our breath at the same time, too.

"We can do this in the living room," she said, not meeting my gaze.

"Lead the way," I said, my voice strained.

CHAPTER THREE

CERYS

I hadn't expected the box to feel so heavy. It wasn't large — just an old cardboard thing with frayed edges and a faded label that had once noted it held 'Fine Welsh Biscuits.' But as I carried it into the living room, it seemed to weigh more with each step.

I set it down on the coffee table. The old table was scratched and stained, a reminder of all the times we'd sat around it, laughing and talking like we had all the time in the world.

Nick hovered in the doorway, hands

shoved deep into his pockets. He looked as uneasy as I felt, his gaze dancing around the room as if searching for an escape route.

"Have you decided to become a coat rack?" I settled on the sofa, fighting the urge to flee myself. "Because if you're planning to loiter there all afternoon, I'll charge rent."

Even scrubbing mould off the ageing racks sounds better than cracking open painful memories. Unfortunately, Meins would never let me hear the end of it if I skipped out.

He cleared his throat and stepped forward. "No. Sorry."

He took a measured step into the room and perched stiffly on the opposite end of the sofa. The distance hurt. I told myself I didn't know why, even though I did.

Before Gareth asked me out in school, I spent an embarrassing amount of time daydreaming that Nick would. I even believed it on the day he approached me, heart pounding, only to find out he was delivering Gareth's message.

Nick's gaze had skimmed over my face, and my heart flared with a wild hope. I thought he'd worked up courage to ask me on a date, perhaps to that silly jazz night at the local pub I'd teased him about. When he uttered Gareth's name instead, something inside me shrivelled. I forced it to the far recesses of my mind, reasoning that at least Gareth wanted me, and he had the courage to ask, even if it was through someone else.

I told myself I'd misread everything. I trained my heart to stop jolting whenever Nick came near. Over time, I convinced myself I'd never wanted him like that.

I prised open the box. A stale paper smell drifted out, carrying hints of old cologne. I inhaled sharply. Gareth's scent. My eyes stung, and my throat tightened.

I snuck a glance at Nick. Nick's gaze drifted towards me, brow furrowing. I clenched my jaw, reluctant to admit we shared this pain. A pang of sympathy consumed me. With all the years of avoidance, sometimes it was hard to remember that he'd lost Gareth too.

But he'd run off to chase his dreams

while I was left to pick up the pieces. The sympathy evaporated, replaced by the familiar bitterness.

I reached inside the box. My fingers closed around a worn ball, the leather scuffed and faded. Eyes already burning with emotion, I turned it over in my hands. "Is this supposed to be a rugby ball, or did Gareth try making cheese behind my back?"

Seriously, the thing was scarred and battered. Some of the air had leaked out over the years, too.

Nick tried for a smile, but it flickered out. "I guess that's what happens when you leave a ball in a barn loft for eight years." His voice had a careful quality, like he was approaching a skittish animal that might bite.

He might not be wrong there. Something dark and ugly had gripped me since he walked in. It wrapped its fingers around my windpipe and squeezed until the emotions I'd spent eight years trying to bury bubbled to the surface with a splutter of anger.

I focused on the ball, flipping it over in

my hands while I wrestled with the incessant need to lash out at him.

"He swore he'd play for Wales one day," I said instead.

We'd laughed when he'd announced that — me calling him delusional, Nick claiming he'd skip every match because he hated exercise. But Gareth's belief in himself had been unshakable.

Now, the cheeky boy I'd once loved was gone, and all we had left were the memories and this box.

"Yeah." Nick pressed his lips into a thin line, his eyes shadowed by an ache he didn't bother to hide. "He dragged me out to the field every weekend, rain or shine."

"Mostly rain." I tried not to smile, but one corner of my mouth betrayed me. "You hated it."

"I hated the mud." He grimaced. "And the bruises. He had a hell of a tackle."

"He never needed much of an excuse to smash you into the ground." I chuckled, the memory easing the grief choking me, along with some of the tension between us. "He was relentless."

Nick scoffed. "He was a rugby fanatic

with terrible aim." That fake smile of his finally gave way to something real, and the haunted look on his face loosened its grip. "He tried to teach me proper form once, and I ended up face-first in a cowpat. You nearly choked laughing."

A genuine laugh slipped out before I could clamp down on it. The sound felt strange, too bright for this dim room. He had always managed to coax laughter from me, even when I wanted to wrap him in nettles. I hated him for having that power. But a flicker of warmth sparked inside me. My chest tightened. I refused to soften. This moment meant nothing.

I set the ball aside. My hand drifted into the box again, and I extracted a stack of ticket stubs bound with a rotting rubber band. Concert mementoes. "Our big collection." I held it out to him.

He slid nearer, arm draping along the sofa's top. The movement brought him into my space. I caught a whiff of soap mingling with wool. A shiver of awareness rippled through me, unbidden and unwelcome.

Oh, fabulous, choose now to acknowledge that

he smells good. Could my body not appreciate something more practical, like a wedge of Caerphilly?

He studied the tickets. "Stereophonics. Iron Maiden. That tiny Welsh indie band you adored. We spent more time at gigs than revising for A-levels." He tapped one stub thoughtfully. "Remember when you got into that mosh pit and emerged with a shiner worthy of a boxing ring?"

I glared at him, though it lacked any real heat. Truth was, I was tired. So very tired. Of the animosity, of tiptoeing around Meins and avoiding my last living best friend. He was supposed to be my shoulder to cry on, the one person I could rely on to pick me up and dust me off once the tear stains had dried.

Stop with the sad thoughts. It only depresses you.

I shook off the melancholy and forced some bite into my voice. "Only because you shoved me into it. Don't rewrite history."

He canted his head, feigning shock. "I saved you from a beer-sloshing maniac who leered at you like you were a cream cake."

I snorted. "Rubbish. You pushed me in so you could impress some girl by acting heroic when rescuing me."

"Credit me with a shred of taste, Evans. Even at eighteen, I knew better than to impress girls by turning my best mate into a punching bag."

I eyed him, sceptical. The laughter tasted bittersweet. I refused to lower my guard. I pointed to another stub.

"That Cardiff gig… Isn't that the one where Gareth tried crowd-surfing and accidentally nearly rearranged your face?"

Okay, so maybe I had ulterior motives bringing that situation up. I needed to keep him talking. Winding him up kept my voice from trembling. If we stuck to funny memories, he wouldn't see my hands shaking or spot the tears in my eyes. Distraction was my shield, a way to keep him from poking at fresh wounds.

Nick snorted, the sound unexpectedly warm. "If by 'accident' you mean he was possessed by some ancient Welsh god of chaos, then yes, absolutely an accident. Thought I'd have to blame the black eye on his sheep to stop Mam's worrying." He glanced at me, eyes warm. "You howled with laughter. Might have been the moment I realised you were more terrifying than the mosh pit."

That earned him a small, involuntary smile from me.

"You deserved worse for pushing me into the mosh pit."

He shifted closer, just enough that if I turned my head, I'd see the stubble along his jaw. The lamplight caught in his dark hair, making it gleam.

"You call it pushing, I call it protecting you from that beer-soaked bloke who kept ogling your ass."

"You can repeat it in as many different ways as you like, I'm never going to believe you." The words came out softer than I wanted.

I needed to keep my guard up. I was supposed to hate him. Nothing had changed. We'd finish going through the box, he'd leave, and I'd never see him again.

Why did the idea of it make my heart plummet to the floor?

To distract myself, I pulled out another item — a slim notebook with the cover half torn off. I sucked in a sharp breath at the sight of Gareth's looping handwriting. He'd scribbled band names, random poetry, and nonsense.

"His lyrics," I said quietly, my fingers tracing the ink.

Nick straightened. "I forgot about that."

"He was always scribbling." I flipped through the pages.

"Hey, some of those were gold." Nick chuckled, the sound low and rumbling. "'Sheep in the Road' was one of my favourites, I'll have you know."

I snorted. "A true masterpiece of rural Welsh life."

"Could've been a hit."

"Maybe with the right marketing." I closed the notebook gently.

Nick chuckled. "He performed it once for us in the barn, remember?"

I laughed, then clamped my mouth shut. Laughter felt almost... treacherous.

Like I was betraying Gareth somehow. My life these past years had been about survival — turning milk into cheese, heartbreak into hardness. Laughter didn't fit into that equation.

Our eyes met, and for a moment, the years between us seemed to fade. I could almost believe we were back in school, plotting our escape to the city.

I pretended not to notice the slight tilt of his head, the way he inhaled when I laughed. I pretended my heartbeat wasn't doing a fandango.

Ridiculous body.

I cleared my throat and reached for another item — crumpled pile of photographs folded at the edges. I slipped them out gently. One image fell onto the table: Gareth with his arms slung around both of us at some music festival. My hair was shorter then, dyed a shade of red I'd thought made me look rebellious. Nick's arm snaked behind me but not quite touching, as if he didn't dare. Gareth bared his teeth in triumph, as if he'd known how bright that moment would burn in our memories.

"This was a good day," I whispered, staring at it.

It was the summer before our final year of school, at the Steelhouse Festival. We'd scraped together enough money for tickets, piling into Gareth's beat-up car for the journey. The entire weekend had been a blur of music, mud, and laughter.

That particular day, we'd managed to sneak our way to the front of the crowd for our favourite band. Gareth had lifted me onto his shoulders and I sang along to every word.

For those few hours, the world had shrunk to just the three of us and the music. It was one of those perfect moments where everything felt possible.

We were young, invincible, and the future stretched out before us like an open road. None of us could have imagined how drastically things would change in just a few short months.

"One of the best." Nick took the photo from me, his fingers brushing mine ever so slightly. The touch sent a jolt through me, sharp and fleeting. I forced myself not to flinch.

"He sweet-talked the security guard into letting us backstage. I still don't understand how." His voice softened. "You yelled every lyric until you went hoarse.

I sighed. "He always could charm his way into anything."

"Except passing maths." Nick chuckled. "You lost your mind a bit that day."

"I did not."

A slow, cocky grin spread across his face, one I wanted to slap right off. "You absolutely did. Especially when he decided to climb the speaker tower and nearly gave the crew a heart attack."

I laughed, surprising us both. "I forgot about that. God, he was such an idiot sometimes."

"Yeah." Nick smiled. "But he was our idiot."

Silence settled between us again, but this time it seemed less oppressive. More like a shared melancholy.

I hated that feeling — the way nostalgia could creep in and soften the edges of my anger. I didn't want to forgive him. Didn't want to let go of the hurt he'd caused.

But surrounded by the remnants of our past, it was hard to hold on to the bitterness.

I pulled out another item — a guitar pick on a frayed cord. Gareth's lucky charm.

"He never went anywhere without this." I held it up so it caught the light.

Nick inhaled sharply. "I'd forgotten about that."

"How could you forget?"

Gareth had been convinced the ratty thing had mystical powers. Though I couldn't really remember when he'd gotten it. It just appeared around his neck the day he found the courage to ask me out.

Nick shrugged. I turned the pick over and traced the faded signature on the back. I squinted at it, my brow wrinkling.

"I can't remember him getting anything signed."

"Actually... it's mine."

I frowned, glancing between him and the pick. He rubbed the back of his neck, giving away his nervousness.

"He borrowed it from me. Said I'd get

it back when I needed it more than he did."

I arched an eyebrow. "He never mentioned that." I turned it over again, a bizarre pang hitting me in the chest. Did Gareth borrow it to ask *me* out? And if so, why did he still have Nick do the asking?

"He probably forgot." Nick's throat bobbed. "Or maybe he thought it was safer with him."

I studied the pick for a moment before holding it out to him. "You should have it back."

He shook his head. "No, it's more a part of his story now. You keep it."

"Are you sure?"

"Yeah. Positive."

I hesitated, swallowing. The idea of wearing something that linked us all together? Dangerous. Too personal. Yet, I still slipped the cord over my head. The pick settled just below my collarbone. My stupid heart fluttered as if I'd swallowed a butterfly whole.

"Thank you."

He nodded, a ghost of a smile dancing on his lips.

"It's just a trinket," I muttered, more to myself than him. "Don't read too much into it."

"Wouldn't dream of it," he said, voice low and his lips curling into that maddening half-smile that made it far too easy to forget everything I hated about him.

I ignored the flutter in my chest and focused instead on the box. My fingers drifted back inside, brushing against something cool and solid. I pulled it out — a set of drumsticks. They were chipped and worn, the paint fading at the edges.

Nick's expression changed instantly. He reached out, expression taut, fingers lingering over old dents and scuffs.

"He gave them to you." Why were they in the box?

Nick nodded, his thumb brushing over one of the scuffed tips. "Yeah. My first pair. He bought them secondhand from that music shop in town when I couldn't afford my own."

I remembered that day. Gareth had been so proud of himself for finding a gift that would mean something to Nick. He'd saved up for weeks, skipping lunch at school and helping his dad with extra chores to afford them.

Nick swallowed hard. "He said they'd help me get where I wanted to go."

"Did that and more, didn't they?" A bitter edge crept back into my tone. "Must feel good."

Nick's head snapped up. "What's that supposed to mean?"

"Nothing." I shoved the sticks into the box, voice sharp. "You know what? Forget it. It doesn't matter."

His jaw clenched, the muscle twitching. "No, I think I want to hear the new accusation you're laying on me."

"It's not an accusation." I sprang to my feet, my hands shaking as the simmering heat of my anger threatened to spill over. "It's just… funny, that's all. Funny how everything worked out perfectly for you. Gareth's gifts, his belief in you — it all paid off, didn't it? And you left it all behind like it was nothing."

"I didn't leave it behind."

"Stop with the bullshit." My voice rose, sharper now. "You can't rewrite history. *You* left."

He left *me.*

He stared at me, his mouth opening like he wanted to fire back, but nothing came. For a second, I thought I'd won, that he'd just sit there and let the weight of what he'd done sink in.

"I miss him too, Cerys. Every day."

It hit me like a slap, his words cutting through the fog of my anger and plunging straight into the ache I'd buried deep inside. Grief rose, hard and fast, turning my stomach and making my eyes burn.

"You *miss* him?" The words were bitter, my voice low and trembling with fury. "You don't get to miss him." My voice cracked at the end, betraying the thin thread of control I had left. Nick opened his mouth, then closed it, looking stricken. Good. Let him scramble for excuses. My fingers trembled. The ache in my chest threatened to buckle my knees. If I stayed here another second, I'd break into sobs.

I couldn't let this spiral, couldn't let him see how close I was to breaking. How easily *he* could break me. The tears were already stinging my eyes, and I refused to let him see them.

He reached out. "Cerys—"

"No." I dodged his outstretched hand. My vision blurred, but I just kept moving.

I couldn't let him see me crumble, couldn't let him think he had the power to pull me under like this.

CHAPTER FOUR

NICK

"Cerys, wait." I followed her out of the living room door and down the corridor. The sight of her running from *me*, twisted something in my gut.

She didn't stop. Of course she didn't. She stormed into the kitchen like she was marching into battle, her braid whipping against her back, her shoulders rigid with tension.

"Talk to me. I want to understand. I want to make it—" — whatever the hell it was — "right."

I barely crossed the threshold before she whirled to face me, her green eyes flashing like the lightning cracking outside the farmhouse. If she'd had a plate in her hand, she might have hurled it at my head.

"Just stop, Nick," she snapped, her voice low and razor-sharp. "I can't do this with you right now."

My first instinct was to argue, to push back, to demand that she tell me what she meant by *this*. But the look on her face — eyes glistening, lips pressed into a thin, trembling line — silenced me.

She didn't want a fight. She wanted me gone.

I clamped my mouth shut. What was the point in arguing? It would only solidify her image of me as the villain who slunk back into town whenever it suited him.

Maybe I'd earned it.

Cerys turned away, leaning over the sink. Water rushed from the tap as she seized a plate, scrubbing it with more force than necessary and plunging it under the running water. The sound of it filled the silence between us, louder than it should have been.

I stuffed my hands into my pockets and just stood there, feeling useless. My foot tapped the worn tile as I just barely resisted the urge to pace.

I felt like a kid again, standing outside the headmaster's office after getting caught sneaking out of school — guilty, embarrassed, and desperately trying to figure out where I'd gone wrong.

I'd said that I missed Gareth, which I did. But why would that set her off? It had to be something else. Something I didn't say maybe? Or was it just my very presence?

But she wasn't supposed to hate me. Not like this. Not with this sharp, biting edge that felt like it was cutting me open every time she looked at me.

"You know, Nick," she said finally, her voice barely audible over the rush of water, "for someone who used to be so dependable, you've gotten damn good at disappointing people."

Talk about a gut punch.

A hollow ache settled behind my ribs. Years ago, I'd have teased her, turned it into a joke that left us both laughing. Now, I just felt the weight of it, heavy and suffocating.

I bit back my instinctive need to snap, defend myself, blame my busy life on the road. What good would that do when part of me agreed with her?

"Let me help." I reached for a towel, desperate for something to do besides stand there absorbing her anger.

She spun, snatching the dishcloth before I could grab it. Our fingers brushed, a bare instant of contact that sent a jolt of awareness spiralling through me. I saw it register in her eyes, too, a flicker of something besides bitterness. Then she yanked her hand away, droplets splattering the flagstones.

"Don't," she said, her knuckles whitening around the cloth. "Just don't."

My throat tightened. "Cerys..."

I winced at how small and unsure it sounded. I wasn't used to this — to feeling this out of my depth. On stage, I knew who I was. I was confident, in control.

"What, Nick?" She stepped closer, her gaze cutting through every defence I had. "What exactly do you think you can fix? You show up after eight years, like missing Gareth's funeral and skipping out on

Meinir's birthday after he died wasn't enough proof you'd washed your hands of us."

My stomach twisted. I'd been in London with the band recording our first tracks. Nothing screwed up carefully laid plans like weather in Wales. A storm had moved in that week and washed out the railway lines. I'd promised myself I'd make it up to them later, but later never came.

"I'm sorry, okay?" The rain outside grew louder, the farmhouse windows rattling under the gusts. "I know I've been gone. I know I didn't call. I don't even know what I said this time that—"

Her laughter cut me off, sharp as shattered glass. "Of course you don't know. You never do, do you? You just breeze in here like nothing's happened, like you haven't spent the last eight years pretending this place doesn't exist."

"That's not fair. I would have been here for you..." Guilt pressed on my lungs. Had Meinir told me about her dad? Did I miss it in a text or a voicemail I never returned? "If I'd known—"

"That's your excuse?" She shook her

head, incredulous. "You didn't know. Because you never asked. Everyone else who cared called, even if they drifted after. You couldn't spare a second for that. Not a funeral, not a birthday, not a five-minute check-in. Nothing."

I wanted to deny it, but I couldn't. Instead, I stared at her with pleading eyes, at a complete loss for words. The silence stretched between us, broken only by the steady patter of rain against the windowpane and the distant rumble of thunder.

All I wanted was to rewind the clock ten minutes, go back into the living room and continue our trip down memory lane. For a little while, it had felt like we were friends again, inseparable.

But even that had flaws, didn't it? It was hard not to think of the bad when we remembered the good. Gareth's memory permeated it all.

"There are phones. People text these days. Call." She gestured to the old, corded phone hanging on Meins's kitchen wall, her voice rising. "Jesus, people have fucking Instagram and God knows what else! Do you know how many of Gareth's mates showed up? Do you? Because I do. And you know what one thing they all did afterward?"

I shook my head, mute, numb, waiting for her to deliver the blow I knew would come. Because what could I say to disagree? She wasn't wrong.

"They fucked off home," she said, her voice trembling with emotion. "But they called. Even if it was just once. But you? Not a word. Not a single bloody word." She shoved the plate she was holding into my hands.

I set it down in the sink and scrubbed a hand over my face. "I don't know what you want me to say. I can't change any of that—"

"No," she said bitterly, "you can't."

"I couldn't..." I closed my eyes, my temples beginning to throb. I'd weathered more than a few fights in my life, but none of them felt this close to breaking something inside of me.

"You couldn't what? Couldn't be bothered? Couldn't spare a day from your precious music career to say goodbye to the people who were supposed to matter to you?"

"That's not fair." My eyes flew open and my hackles rose, a familiar mix of guilt and anger bubbling up. "You have no idea what I was going through. What I'm still going through."

She laughed, a harsh, bitter sound. "Oh, poor Nick. It must be so hard being a big rock star. All those adoring fans, all that money. How do you cope?"

"You don't know what you're talking about," I snapped, anger overriding my better judgment. "Try living out of a suitcase for months on end. Try having every move you make scrutinised and judged."

"Cry me a river," she spat.

Hurt glimmered in her eyes, raw and accusing, and it made me want to reach out to her. But I knew I had no right.

"I never wanted to hurt anyone," I said, my anger deflating as quickly as it had come. "I just... I couldn't face it. Any of it. So I ran."

"You're still running," she said, her voice low and intense. "You show up here, acting like nothing's changed, like you can just waltz back into our lives—"

"I never said that!" I shouted, but even to my own ears, it sounded weak. I ran a hand through my hair, frustration building. "Christ, Cerys, do you think this is easy for me? I miss him every fucking day. I see his face every time I close my eyes."

My hand unconsciously moved to my left arm, tracing the outline of the tattoo hidden beneath my sleeve. The Welsh dragon, intertwined with a treble clef — a permanent reminder of where I came from and what I'd lost.

She flinched at that, and I saw a flicker of something — understanding? Sympathy? — in her eyes. But it was gone in an instant, replaced by that same hard anger.

"I didn't mean to—" I started, but she cut me off.

She gripped a plate so hard I feared it would crack. "If you really missed Gareth" —her voice faltered on his name, eyes shining with more than anger—"you'd have shown up. If you meant what you said about him being your best friend, you wouldn't have run. You wouldn't have forgotten him and acted like he never existed."

"I didn't forget," I said, my voice low and strained. "I could never forget."

"Could've fooled me," she muttered.

"I'm serious." Shame formed a tight knot in my chest. "I was drowning in guilt. So much so that I wrote a song about him trying to deal with the pain."

Cerys froze, surprise flickering across her face.

"I never played it for anyone, not even the band. It hurt too much." I took a step forward, closing the distance between us until she had to tip her head back or retreat.

She stared into my eyes with a vulnerability that both terrified and captivated me. Just like that, the years melted away, and I was seventeen again. Heart pounding in my chest, palms sweaty, pulse pounding in my throat stealing my voice.

A stray lock of black hair fell across her cheek, and I ached to reach out and tuck it behind her ear. God, what was wrong with me?

After everything, after all the silence

and the mess I'd made, how could I still crave even the smallest touch? I had no right.

My gaze drifted over her face, taking in every change time had carved into it — the sharper angles of her cheekbones, the tension around her eyes, the way her jaw tightened as if holding back a thousand words she refused to speak. She wasn't the carefree, optimistic girl I remembered, the one who'd once laughed when I drummed on tabletops or teased me about my dodgy Welsh slang. She'd hardened, grown guarded.

And yet something underneath that hardness still drew me in, like I was fourteen again and hopelessly smitten, but preparing to give her up because Gareth called dibs first.

Wanting her was a joke now, a cruel punchline to the life I'd lived on the road, always running from home. But it didn't stop my stomach from twisting at the scent of her or wishing she'd smile at me like she used to. It didn't stop me from noticing how her lashes trembled ever so slightly when she blinked, or how that single strand of hair refused to stay put, as if daring me to do something about it.

I stared back at her, tongue-tied, feeling that old ache flare back to life. And it hurt, knowing that I couldn't make a move even if I wanted to. She would always be Gareth's girl. It hurt worse knowing I wanted her anyway, even if she hated me, even if I deserved every scrap of anger in her voice.

"I wasn't running from *him*," I whispered.

"Right. It was the rest of us you couldn't wait to escape," she muttered, her tone dry.

I ran a hand through my hair, frustration building. "I didn't mean it like that. You know that."

"No, I really don't."

As if on cue, another clap of thunder echoed outside, rolling slowly over the fields and pulling her gaze away from me.

"You think an apology or a secret sad song will fix anything? My dad's gone. Gareth's gone." A flash of lightning lit the kitchen, turning the shadows stark. Cerys inhaled sharply, and for a breath, I thought

I saw tears. "Meinir barely talks about him anymore. And I'm here, holding it all together. Meanwhile, you're living your dream, unaffected."

"That is not true."

What did I have to do to make her hear me?

I closed the distance again, aware on some level that I shouldn't crowd her — that it would only make it worse — but I couldn't stop. We were toe-to-toe now, close enough that I could see the faint freckles dusting her nose, smell the lingering scent of milk and herbs that clung to her clothes.

No, no, no. Back away, you idiot. She's not yours. She'll never be yours.

But I couldn't. It was like some magnetic pull I was powerless to resist. My traitorous body leaned in, inch by agonising inch, drawn to her like a moth to a flame.

My gaze dropped to lips I'd spent far too long trying not to think about. Lips that, even now, made my gut twist with sheer longing. I inhaled sharply as the urge to close the distance built in me. My heart raced, pounding so loudly I was sure she could hear it.

Move. Back away.

"Cerys," I whispered, her name a fragile thing on my lips, tangled with years of unspoken words and buried desires. The kitchen seemed to fade away, leaving just the two of us, teetering on the edge of something dangerous and thrilling.

And for one brief, dizzying moment, she leaned in. Time seemed to slow, each second stretching out like taffy, the distance shrinking, the years of separation dissolving.

My gaze drifted to her lips again, full and slightly parted, and a wave of longing washed over me, so intense it nearly stole my breath.

But then she blinked, and reality crashed in.

I almost kissed her.

The realisation slammed into me like a physical blow, stealing the air from my lungs. Guilt, thick and suffocating, coiled in my chest.

What the hell was wrong with me? I was a selfish bastard, plain and simple.

I stepped back, putting the island between us. I needed to leave. Staying had been a mistake.

"I can't do this," I bit out, my voice thick with emotion. And then I did what I had always done best.

I turned and walked out.

"Of course," Cerys called after me, her voice sharp enough to cut glass. "Go ahead. Run back to your precious band. It's not like you've made a habit of sticking around."

Her words hit me like a blow, but I didn't turn around. Couldn't. Because if I did, the weight of everything — the guilt, the loss, the years of distance — would break me. I stormed down the hallway, my footsteps echoing loudly on the worn floorboards.

I yanked open the front door with a finality that felt too predictable, too easy. The old hinges creaked in protest.

I froze.

Rain hammered down in sheets so thick that the world beyond the doorstep was just a swirling mess of grey. Large puddles had already formed in the yard. A low rumbling sound in the distance told me it wasn't just a passing shower.

It was a bloody flash flood.

Of course. Because the universe, like Meins, had a twisted sense of humour.

"Shit." I'd been too inside my own head to realise just how bad things had gotten outside. The wind whipped around me, sending icy droplets of rain that stung against my face.

Lightning flashed, illuminating the flooded yard for a brief, blinding moment. In its wake, thunder crashed overhead, so loud it seemed to shake the very foundations of the house.

"What's wrong?" Cerys asked behind me, her voice a mix of lingering anger and reluctant concern. "Forgot how to open an umbrella, rock star?"

I turned to face her, watching as her expression shifted from annoyance to shock as she took in the scene beyond the door. Her eyes widened, and for a moment, all the tension between us was forgotten in the face of this new, shared predicament.

"Oh," she breathed, her anger seemingly evaporating as quickly as it had flared. "That's... not good."

A humourless laugh escaped me. "Yeah, you could say that."

The wind surged, rattling the door in my hand, whistling through the house. The driveway had all but disappeared under a sheet of water.

We were trapped.

CHAPTER FIVE

CERYS

"How bad is it?" Nick asked.

The ancient computer whirred and clicked, its fan struggling against the damp air as I refreshed the weather page for what felt like the hundredth time. Outside, the storm raged on, a relentless beast of wind and rain that battered against the farmhouse windows.

"Fuck," I muttered, my fingers drumming an anxious rhythm on the worn desk.

The room smelled of damp wood and musty papers, the scent of an old house caught in the grip of a storm it wasn't quite ready for. Much like me, really.

Nick hovered over my shoulder, close enough that I could feel the heat radiating off his body. It was distracting, to say the least. I fought the urge to lean into him, to seek comfort in his familiar presence.

Old habits die hard, I suppose.

"That bad, huh?" His voice was low, tinged with worry.

I kept my eyes fixed on the screen, afraid of what I might do if I looked at him. Our last argument still rang in my ears, the finality of it all threatening to suffocate me.

"Worse," I said, clicking through the tabs on the weather site. Each report was bleaker than the last, thresholds blinking an angry red. "The river's already breached, and it's not showing any signs of stopping."

Nick shifted beside me, and I could practically feel the tension rolling off him. It was almost funny how in tune I still was with his moods, even after all these years. I pushed down the warmth that threatened to bloom in my chest at the thought.

Instead, I glanced out the window, watching as the storm began to devour everything I knew. Meins's fields were shrinking under the weight of the water. Some of the lower-lying sections had already disappeared completely.

"We're surrounded," I said, more to myself than to Nick. "No getting out tonight."

"Fuck." He blew out a long, frustrated breath. His hands clenched and un-clenched at his sides. "I really don't have time for this."

I turned my head and glared at him. "What's that supposed to mean?"

"This," he waved towards the window, his gesture encompassing not just the storm, but the entire farm. "I have plans. Commitments. Important ones."

"You think I don't? Meinir built this place from nothing. She deserves to know her home isn't about to wash away."

Before he could respond, his phone buzzed. He glanced at the screen, his jaw tightening. "Just a minute," he muttered, stalking off to the far corner of the study.

I watched him go, noting how his shoulders tensed as he answered the call.

Even from across the room, I could hear the voice on the other end exploding from the speaker, a mixture of panic and disbelief.

"What the fuck did that text mean, man? You can't miss this!"

"I know, Tommy." Nick ran a hand through his hair. "But there's a bloody flash flood, and I'm stuck at the farm. I might not make it back for the gig."

My teeth ground together as I listened. Of course it was about the band. It was always about the band with Nick.

Tommy's voice crackled through the phone again. "What do you mean stuck?"

Nick's voice became more measured, but I could hear the underlying fear. "It's the last thing I want, but you need to find a backup drummer just in case."

He turned, catching my eye for the briefest of moments. My stomach did a little flip, a confusing sensation given my rising frustration. I turned back to the computer screen, trying to focus on the reports instead of the way Nick paced.

He hadn't stopped moving, but the

movement was all wrong — too jerky, too quick, like he was wound too tight to stand still. Every few steps, his phone buzzed again, and each time, his hand clenched tighter around it before he swiped it silent.

He was spiralling. Not in some loud, over-the-top way, but in that quiet, frantic way I remembered from when things got overwhelming in school. It grated on me to see him like this now, knowing I'd have to step in if it didn't stop.

I didn't want to be the one to ground him.

Not after everything.

The whole room felt smaller with him in it, his panic pressing against everything.

I picked up my phone and slipped out of the study, dialling one of the farmhands as I went.

"Cerys, my love. I'd say it's good to hear from you, but I have a feeling this isn't a social call."

I winced at the teasing note in his voice. Declan had hit on me more times than I could count over the years, but I'd always turned him down. Still, he never seemed to lose hope.

"No, it's not. That thunderstorm's turning into a full on flood."

"Aye, I see it," Declan gruff voice crackled through the line. "We already secured the equipment."

"Oh, good. What about the sheep? Are they on higher ground today?"

"Not yet, but we'll sort it."

For a fraction of a second, I relaxed. "Great, thank you. Be careful out there."

"Don't you worry about us. We'll get it done."

I ended the call and immediately dialled Meins.

"Cerys, cariad! Are you alright?" Meinir's voice was warm with concern.

"I'm fine, Meins. Just checking you're safe. Where are you?"

"Oh, I'm at Malcolm's in town. High and dry, don't you worry."

I breathed a sigh of relief. "Good. We've got everything under control here."

There was a pause, and I could practically hear the slyness in Meinir's voice when she spoke again. "And how are things with you and Nicky?"

I rolled my eyes. "Really, Meins? That's what you're worried about right now?"

"Well, a little flood never hurt anyone. But you two... have you made any progress?"

I lowered my voice, just in case Nick walked in. "Look, I know what you're trying to do, but you've misread the entire situation. Nick doesn't want me. He's made that pretty clear."

She chuckled. "Oh, cariad. I may be old, but I'm not blind. That boy looks at you the same way he did when you were teenagers."

"You're seeing things that aren't there," I said, but I couldn't ignore the way my heart skipped at her words.

I hung up, shaking my head. As if Nick and I could ever... No. It was better not to even think about it.

I walked back into the study and found Nick still pacing, each lap of the room quicker than the last. His hair was dishevelled, likely from running his hands through it repeatedly, and his boots clunked against the creaky wooden floor, the sound grating on my already frayed nerves.

He hung up his call, but he didn't stop moving. His shoulders were drawn so tight it looked like he might snap, his eyes darting to the window, the desk, the phone still buzzing in his hand.

"Everything alright?" I asked, trying to keep my voice neutral.

Nick glanced up, his blue eyes stormy with worry. "Not really. The label exec is in town. If I miss this gig..." He trailed off, resuming his pacing with renewed vigour.

I watched him for a moment, torn between sympathy and frustration. We were in the middle of a crisis, and all he could fixate on was his career? But then again, wasn't I doing the same with the farm?

I clenched my jaw, fighting the urge to snap at him. Maybe it wasn't fair to expect him to handle this the way I would. But watching him unravel, with all that restless energy and nowhere to put it, made something inside me twist.

The Nick I remembered was calm, steady, always in control. Seeing him like this was... unsettling. And infuriating. Because now, I had to be the one to steady him, whether I wanted to or not.

He finally stopped, sighing heavily. "This gig could change everything for us."

"Is your rock star life more important than people's safety?" I couldn't keep the bitterness out of my voice. "Because really, what are your options? If you go out there, you're just pulling the emergency services away from helping people who actually need saving."

He spun to face me, his eyes flashing. "It's not that simple, Cerys."

"It's always that simple with you, isn't it?" I crossed my arms, meeting his gaze squarely. "You disappear for months, chasing your dreams, but when it really matters here, to the people who actually gave a damn about you before... you're nowhere to be found."

His face twisted, a mix of guilt and anger flashing across his features. "That's not fair."

I laughed, the sound harsh even to my own ears. "Right. Because you've never let anyone down for a gig before." The words tasted bitter as they spilled out, but I couldn't stop them. Not now.

His eyes narrowed, and he took a step towards me. "If you want to get into all that again..."

"Actually, I don't," I cut him off. "What I do want is to stop the house from being flooded out while you sulk."

"I'm not sulking," he growled, closing the distance between us.

He was close enough now that I could smell his cologne, a mix of citrus and spice that made my head spin.

"And I said it's not that simple, alright? I want to help." He drove a hand through his hair again, and I hated how attractive I still found the gesture.

"I need you to stop panicking and... and..." I paused, letting my eyes roam over him deliberately. "...and maybe put that gym-bro body to some actual use."

He blinked, clearly caught off guard by my sudden change in tone. "What, uh... what do you need me to do?"

"Sandbags," I said abruptly, brushing past him. The brief contact sent a jolt through me, and I hoped he couldn't hear how my shoulders stiffened. "You remember how to handle that, don't you?"

Nick followed close behind, his presence a constant, maddening awareness at my back. "Yeah, I'll do whatever you need."

CHAPTER SIX

NICK

Another sandbag landed with a wet thud, the damp hessian scratching against my bare arms. Rain lashed down, plastering my hair to my forehead and turning the grass surrounding the house into a muddy swamp.

Cerys trudged past, a sandbag hoisted over her shoulder as if it weighed nothing. She was stronger than she looked. I pitied any guy who tried to insert himself between her and a difficult task.

I grabbed another sandbag, and my muscles burned, but I wasn't about to let Cerys outpace me. Not that she'd noticed.

She moved with single-minded determination, barely sparing me a glance as she dumped her bag onto the growing wall around the front door.

Rain dripped from the tip of her nose, her braid clinging to her back. Mud streaked her jeans, but she didn't seem to care. She paused, hands on her hips, surveying the barrier like a general inspecting her troops.

"We'll need another layer," she said, her voice cutting through the downpour.

I grunted, hefting my bag onto the pile. "You planning to build a fortress? Or just a moat to keep the villagers out?"

She shot me an unamused look. "You got a better idea?"

"Not really." I wiped the rain from my eyes. "But if we're going to keep this up, I might need a snack. Or a stretcher."

Her lips twitched, almost a smile, but she quickly turned away. "Keep moving, rock star. The rain's not going to wait for you to finish your stand-up routine."

I followed her back to the pile, my boots squelching in the mud. The ground was a mess, slick and treacherous, and more than once I had to catch myself before I ended up flat on my back. Cerys, of course, moved like she'd been born in the stuff.

She always had a knack for this sort of thing. When we were kids, Gareth and I used to grumble through every chore, while Cerys tackled them head-on, like she thrived on the challenge. She'd race us to see who could fill the most sandbags or stack the hay bales fastest. And, without fail, she'd win. Every damn time.

Now, even with the years apart and all the anger simmering between us, that same determination blazed in her eyes. Meanwhile, I was just trying to keep up.

"Have you beaten your record yet?" I asked, grabbing another bag.

Cerys glanced at me, her brow furrowing. "What record?"

"From the '07 flood." I adjusted the bag on my shoulder, pretending the weight didn't bother me. "Gareth swore you cheated."

Her lips twitched, a flicker of amusement breaking through her stormy expression. "He was just mad he couldn't keep up."

"Probably. He did call you 'the machine' for weeks after that." I chuckled. "Not that he ever said it to your face." He'd been too scared she'd knock him flat on his ass.

She smirked and slammed her sandbag into place. "He should've been scared. I earned that name."

"Not arguing," I muttered, dropping my bag on top of hers. The wall was coming together, uneven but solid.

We'd done this so many times as kids, it felt like muscle memory kicking in. Well, for her. Every muscle in my body was gearing up to stage a protest.

"You're slower than I remember."

"I'm pacing myself." I leaned against the house wall, taking a second to find my balance. "Not everyone can be a one-woman flood defence."

She didn't dignify that with a response. Instead, she turned on her heel and trudged away from the pile, heading towards the shed where the rest of the sandbags were stored.

I sighed. She had to be part cyborg. There was no other explanation for how she kept going without so much as a grunt of complaint. I'd barely caught my breath before she disappeared around the corner, and with a groan, I forced my legs to follow.

The rain was relentless, each drop slamming into me like it had a grudge to settle. My boots stuck in the mud with every step, threatening to trap me if I slowed down too much.

By the time we got back to the barrier, the pile of sandbags looked like it was holding its own against gravity. Cerys didn't pause to admire the work, though. She dropped her bag into place and went straight for another, her focus razor-sharp.

"You planning to take a nap back there?" Cerys called out what felt like hours later. She'd beaten me to the shed yet again and was bent over one of the pallets of sandbags. She didn't bother turning around.

"Yeah, thought I'd just lie down in the mud and let the storm finish me off."

The end had to be in sight. Right?

We'd already finished the front of the house. Now we were adding some precautionary bags to the back door, but that had never been at risk of flooding in the past.

"Sounds about right," she said, her tone dry as the Sahara.

I grabbed a bag off the pallet, hefting it onto my shoulder with a grunt. "You know, some people ease into this kind of thing."

She turned to me, one brow arched. "Some people aren't made for it."

I smirked. "Ouch. You trying to hurt my feelings, Evans?"

"If you had feelings, maybe." She pivoted and started back towards the house, her pace unrelenting.

I muttered something under my breath about stubborn women and followed her, the weight of the sandbag digging into my shoulder. It was almost nostalgic, in a miserable kind of way.

I couldn't resist turning to watch her walk away. Don't ask me why, but there had always been something about the way she moved that captivated me.

"You're going to burn yourself out at this rate," I called after her.

She didn't break stride. "I'm not the one wheezing like a geriatric."

The words were clipped, and the edge in her tone left no room for argument.

"Easy for you to say." I clutched my side. If I didn't know any better, I'd say she was fuelled by spite.

"Just trying to finish this before the flood sweeps us both away." She dropped the bag. "The faster you move, the faster we're done."

"Ah, so you can get inside and hog all the hot water?"

She spun to face me with an obnoxiously innocent expression. "Would I do that to you?"

"Absolutely," I said, without hesitation. "You'd leave me with the ice-cold dribble and laugh about it for days."

Her lips twitched, but she didn't give me the satisfaction of a smile. Instead, she walked away. "Well, maybe if you moved a bit faster, you'd get there first."

"Is that a challenge?" I asked, dropping the sandbag from my shoulder. My muscles were already screaming, but there was no way I was backing down now.

She tilted her head, eyes narrowing. "It's a fact. You're dragging, Nick. You've gone soft."

CERYS

Nick froze, his gaze narrowing, and a mean little flicker of satisfaction danced through me.

Good. Let him squirm.

The corner of his mouth twitched, but his eyes stayed sharp. I started walking. Partly because I really was freezing and the thought of a hot shower sounded like heaven, and partly to get away from him. I wasn't sure how much longer I could stop my eyes from devouring every soaking wet, defined inch of the man.

There was nothing soft about him.

He followed me, releasing a low chuckle that skirted up my spine to tease my hormones.

"You really think I've gone soft?"

"You tell me."

I didn't look at him. Didn't dare.

In school, needling him had been a sport, something to fill the afternoons between chores. Now it wasn't just about seeing him squirm. I used to wish he'd notice me the way Gareth did, the way I'd catch myself noticing him when I shouldn't have. And the worst part? He still had that stupid effect on me, even now.

I put extra stomp in my steps as I power walked back to the shed, clenching my fingers against the urge to kiss the stupid smug quirk from his lips and claw his pointless shirt off while I was at it.

God help me.

I'd spent so long burying those feelings, I didn't have the first clue how to handle them now.

Lusting after a man who hated me. Could I be any more pathetic?

Probably not, but self-pity wasn't going to help me get through this. I reached the shed, yanked another sandbag off the stack, and slung it over my shoulder with more force than necessary. The hessian scratched against my neck, and I welcomed the discomfort — it gave me something to focus on besides the man trailing behind me.

Maybe if I focused hard enough, I could shut him out. Not just his voice, but everything about him — his stupid grin, the way his shoulders moved under that soaked-through shirt, and the way my chest ached when I remembered how we used to be.

"You're awfully quiet over there." Nick hefted his bag into place beside mine.

I didn't look at him. "I've learned the value of silence. You should try it sometime."

"Now, that's just unfair. You didn't used to mind me talking. Used to laugh at my jokes, even."

I took a step back, my gaze shifting to anything but him. "Yeah, well, people change."

"Do they?" His tone was light, but his words hooked into something deeper, making me glance at him despite myself.

His eyes met mine, steady and searching, and for a moment, I couldn't breathe. There was something unguarded and raw. It wasn't the smug defiance I was used to, nor the practised charm he wore like a second skin. This was... vulnerable in a way that made my chest ache.

I hated it. Not because it wasn't genuine, but because it was. Because for the first time in years, it felt like he was asking me a question I didn't know how to answer. One that I wasn't sure I wanted to answer.

I forced out a laugh, the sound sharper than I intended, and looked away. If I didn't, I was afraid I'd start believing whatever it was he wasn't saying.

"Some of us had to."

I didn't give him a chance to respond. I turned tail and got the hell out of there. The shed felt too small, too enclosed, the air thick with the storm outside and something heavier between us.

The downpour was a relief, the cold washing over me as I trudged back towards the barricade. Anything was better than being stuck in there with his stupid voice and stupid face — both of which had been haunting me long before he showed up again.

"You know, Evans," Nick called after me, not taking the hint, "if you're going to stomp away like that, you could at least tell me what the hell that was supposed to mean."

I didn't stop. "It means exactly what it sounded like."

The sandbag on my shoulder started to slide and I picked up my pace. He swore and the sound of his steps increased.

"Great, so I've got to decode your riddles now? Or is this just a game where you make me guess how badly I've screwed up this time?"

"You're not that thick. You'll figure it out."

We neared the back door barricade, and I shifted the bag higher, ignoring the ache in my arms. The last thing I wanted was to drop it and have Nick jump in to save the day.

I dumped the sandbag onto the top row. Swiping at my face, I stepped back to survey the wall. It wasn't pretty, but it'd hold. For now. The rain hammered down, plastering my braid to my back and soaking through my clothes. Mud clung to every inch of me, and my jeans felt heavy enough to pull me straight into the ground.

"Nice work," he said, his voice annoyingly casual, like we were painting a fence instead of trying to keep the floodwaters out. "I'd say we're about ready to start our own flood defence business. Evans and Davies, sandbaggers for hire."

I snorted, mostly to keep myself from smiling. "That'll look great on your CV. Professional mud wrestler, part-time drummer."

Nick crossed his arms defiantly, as if he weren't drenched to the bone and shivering from the cold. "At least I'd have a fallback. What's your excuse?"

"My excuse," I said, turning to face him, "is that I don't need one. This is my life, not a backup plan."

Something flickered across his face, too quick to read. He opened his mouth, but before he could say anything, his boot slipped.

One second he was standing there,

cocky grin intact. The next, he was falling, arms flailing like a wind-up toy that had run out of juice. He landed flat on his back in the mud.

The sound he made — a mix between a grunt and a curse — was so absurd that I couldn't help it. I laughed. Hard.

It started as a chuckle, but the sight of him sprawled out in the muck, looking like a drowned cat, pushed me over the edge. My sides ached as I doubled over, the laughter bubbling up uncontrollably.

"Glad I could brighten your day," he muttered, attempting to push himself up but slipping again. "Real supportive. Great friend you are."

I tried to respond, but the words wouldn't come. The laughter had taken over, shaking me so hard I nearly lost my balance. Was this a mental breakdown? Had the stress finally cracked me like one of the overripe Brie wheels I'd lost in the last flood?

And then, because the universe clearly had it out for me, my boot caught in the same patch of mud, and I went down too.

Right on top of him.

My hands slapped against his chest, his soaked shirt clinging to the solid muscles underneath. One knee wedged awkwardly between his thighs, dangerously close to delicate territory. His arms instinctively wrapped around me, steadying us both, his palms warm even through the cold rain and layers of fabric.

The impact sent a jolt through both of us. We froze, the world narrowing to the sharp intake of his breath and the steady thud of his heart beneath my fingers.

Oh, God.

Did I just knee him?

Nope. Close, but no direct hit.

My cheeks burning, I forced myself to meet his gaze.

Big mistake.

His attention was locked on mine, intense and unyielding, his pupils blown wide enough to swallow the stormy blue. I was acutely aware of every point of contact — his hands at my waist, the damp fabric of his shirt against my palms, the way my braid dripped water onto his neck.

"Comfortable?" he asked, his voice low

and the teasing edge softened by a note that made my pulse stutter.

I opened my mouth to respond, but the words got stuck between my brain and my tongue. The smart thing to do would've been to scramble off him, mutter some half-assed apology, and move on.

But I didn't.

I couldn't.

Because I was drowning in the way he was looking at me — like I was the only thing in the world that mattered.

I should move.

I should say something.

Instead, I leaned in closer, drawn by some magnetic force I didn't fully under-stand. A muscle ticked in his jaw, his grip tightening ever so slightly on my waist, and for a split second, I thought...

No. Don't be stupid, Cerys.

But the thought wouldn't be silenced, it overpowered sense, added extra weight to the undeniable urge to close the distance between us. Eight years of anger, hurt, and unspoken words melted away under the heat of his gaze.

I swallowed hard. "We've done all we can out here."

His brow creased, confusion flickering across his face. Then realisation dawned, softening the edges of his expression. His lips parted just enough to make my stomach flip.

"We should clean up." I struggled to push the words past the tightness in my throat. My pulse pounded in my ears, loud enough to drown out the rain, and I wondered if he could hear it too.

His hands loosened their grip on me, the warmth of his touch still lingering. But he didn't let go entirely.

"Clean up?"

My lungs locked up at the edge of curiosity in those two words.

"Yeah."

I pushed myself up, only to realise that I was now straddling him, my body pressed intimately against his. I could feel the heat of him through our clothes, and a shiver ran through me that had nothing to do with the cold. He was semi-hard beneath me, and the knowledge sent a rush of courage mixed with embarrassment coursing through my veins.

For years, I'd locked away every stolen glance, every flicker of something I wasn't supposed to feel for him. It had felt wrong back then — like wanting him was some kind of betrayal to Gareth.

But now, every carefully constructed wall I'd built crumbled. He wasn't Gareth's best friend anymore, wasn't the boy I'd forbidden myself from wanting.

He was just Nick.

And God, I wanted him.

I glanced down at him, expecting a smirk, some cocky comment to puncture the tension crackling between us. Instead, his face was unreadable, the storm in his eyes dark and deep, pulling me in.

Neither of us moved, and the rain continued to pelt down, plastering my hair to my face and running in rivulets over his skin.

"You going to say something, or are we just going to sit here until we both catch pneumonia?"

His lips twitched. "I'm thinking about it. Give me a second."

"You're going to need more than that to come up with something halfway clever," I scoffed, though the waver in my voice betrayed me.

"You'd be surprised," he said, his voice rougher than usual. His gaze flicked to my lips before snapping back to my eyes, and my heart stuttered.

What the hell was I doing?

He'll be gone in the morning. What does it matter?

True.

I'd let him go, but not before I took something for myself.

Screw restraint. Screw doing what was expected. I wanted this. I wanted him.

For once, I wasn't going to think about tomorrow.

CHAPTER SEVEN

NICK

The front door slammed shut behind us as we trudged into the mudroom, leaving footprints in our wake. Every step felt like dragging dead weight. My body ached from the hours of hauling sandbags and fighting against the storm. Cold sweat mingled with the rain that had soaked through my clothes, and I was pretty sure I smelled worse than a wet dog at this point.

Christ, I needed a shower.

Cerys peeled her soaked jacket off, her hair plastered to her forehead in damp tendrils. She was just as covered in grime as me. If I hadn't taken that rookie fall at the end, she might have won that competition. Not that a bit of dirt did anything to dim her appeal. Even scowling, the woman took my breath away.

"Ugh, I'm going to smell like a sheep dipped in cow shit if I don't get out of these clothes."

A glint of determination flashed in her eyes as she tossed the jacket onto the floor with a wet splat. The same look she'd gotten on her face before she'd called time on the torture session. Before she'd forced herself to her feet and removed her delectable body from mine.

The way she fit against me, her warmth seeping into my skin, would forever be burned into my brain. I'd been so caught up in the heat of her touch that I could have happily stayed there, lying in the mud, if it meant she wouldn't let go.

I glanced down at my mud-covered jeans. "I'm right there with you. I don't think I've ever been this dirty."

Cerys snorted, wiping a streak of mud

off her cheek with the back of her hand. "Well, that's what happens when you play farmer for a couple of hours, rock star."

I rolled my eyes, kicking off my boots. "You're never going to let that go, are you?"

"Not a chance." She shot me a sideways glance, her lips quirking up in a half-smile. "Besides, you're the one who said you wanted to help."

"The way I remember it, you didn't give me a choice."

Cerys paused, her hands stilling on the hem of her shirt. She looked at me, her eyes flashing with a mix of amusement and defiance. "Oh, please. You were driving me mad with all that pacing. I figured I might as well put your anxious energy to good use. Consider it life experience."

"Yeah, well, life experience doesn't usually leave me smelling like I've been rolling around in a barn."

Cerys shrugged, already unbuttoning her flannel shirt. "Welcome to my world."

I wasn't sure if it was the exhaustion or the fact that we were both filthy, but it felt like the tension between us had simmered down — at least for the moment. Which was good, considering I didn't have the energy to go for round three with her right then. All I wanted was a shower.

Cerys glanced towards the hallway. "There's only enough hot water for one shower," she said matter-of-factly. "And since I'm not about to sit around freezing while you take your sweet time, we'll just share."

I blinked, sure I'd misheard her. "What?"

"You heard me, rock star." She turned her back to me as she struggled to yank off her muddy jeans. "We share, or I go first, and you get what's left — if anything."

I watched transfixed as she revealed more skin, my breath hitching uncontrollably.

"You're serious?" My brain scrambled to keep up, every logical thought drowned out by the image of her naked under the spray, soap gliding over her skin. I swallowed hard. "You're not just messing with me?"

"Not everything's a joke." Her lips curled, a ghost of amusement flickering across her face as she finally managed to get one leg free. "Unless you're scared?"

Finally free of her jeans, she levelled a no-nonsense stare at me. It didn't seem to occur to her that she stood in front of me wearing nothing but a thin strap top and lacy underwear. Forget keeping the beat in front of eighty-thousand people, not ogling her was harder.

What were we talking about?

Right, the shower.

I let out a nervous laugh, dragging a hand through my hair. "Scared of a little water? Please."

"Okay then, shall we?" She gestured to the empty hallway.

I didn't move. Wasn't sure I could.

Cerys raised an eyebrow, her lips twitching into a smirk. "Don't overthink it, rock star. It's just a shower."

Just a shower. Right.

Totally normal. Two old friends — well, sort of friends — sharing a shower because the world outside was literally flooding and we both smelled like shit. Nothing weird about that at all.

"Right," I said, trying to sound nonchalant. "Just a shower."

Her smirk widened, and she tossed her jeans into the growing pile of muddy clothes. "Let's get this over with, then."

She brushed past me, heading down the hallway towards the main bathroom. I couldn't do more than watch her for a second, my heart pounding, heat prickling at the back of my neck as I tried to wrap my head around what the fuck just happened.

She'd spent the better part of the day glaring daggers at me and made it abundantly clear that she could barely stand to be in the same room as me. And now, she was agreeing to share a shower?

What the hell was happening?

She was off-limits, no matter how much I wanted her — then and now. Yet desire still unfurled inside of me, a pull so strong it made my hands shake.

This is a bad idea. A terrible idea.

But as I watched her disappear into the bathroom, I knew I wasn't strong enough to walk away this time. I followed her, my mind racing as I tried to figure out how to play this without making it weird.

Not that it wasn't already weird. But still. There was a way to handle this, right? Like two normal, mature adults who had absolutely no unresolved sexual tension between them.

Except we did.

And it was thick enough to choke on.

Cerys pushed open the bathroom door and flicked on the light, revealing the small, tiled space. The shower head hung over an old clawfoot bathtub, a curtain pulled back to reveal the porcelain. It wasn't huge, but it was big enough for two people — if those two people didn't mind standing very, very close together.

I swallowed hard, trying to ignore the knot of anticipation tightening in my gut.

"Well?" she said, glancing at me in the mirror. "You gonna stand there all day, or are we doing this?"

I shook myself out of my daze and stepped into the bathroom, closing the door behind me. The click of the latch sounded louder than it should have, and I tried not to think about how small the space had suddenly become.

"Right," I said, rubbing the back of

my neck. "Let's, uh... let's get this over with."

Cerys snorted and reached for the hem of her strap top, whisking it over her head in one smooth motion. My gaze immediately dropped to the curve of her back, mesmerised by the play of muscles as she sent the shirt flying into the hamper. Then she turned the shower on, leaning over the bath while she fiddled with the temperature. Her lace clad ass swayed in front of me, and I didn't have a hope in hell of tearing my gaze away.

"You're such a tease," I muttered, turning away and silently scolding myself for being an idiot.

This wasn't supposed to be a big thing. Just a shower, two people cleaning up after a long day of working in the mud. No big deal.

But my brain didn't get the memo. All I could think about was the fact I was about to get into a very tight space with a very naked Cerys.

"Grow up, prude."

I turned back, words of denial clamouring to the tip of my tongue.

Big mistake.

She straightened, satisfied with the water temperature. A light, teasing laugh escaped her lips, sending a flip through my stomach. With a smirk, she let her underwear fall to the floor, then unclasped her bra. She tossed it my way before stepping into the shower.

"What the...?"

I stared at the lacy fabric dangling from my fingers, my mind blank. It was still warm, clinging to the memory of her body. I couldn't help but run my finger over the intricate pattern, imagining the softness of her skin beneath, the way her nipples might harden at the touch of my tongue through the thin, almost non-existent material.

"You planning on fondling my bra all day?"

"I'm not," I said, my gravelly voice giving me away.

I dropped the bra into the hamper and quickly unbuttoned my own shirt, shrugging it off and tossing it aside. The cool air hit my skin, making the hairs on my arms stand on end as I reached for my waistband. I yanked off my jeans and boxers in one go, kicking them into the corner and stepping towards the shower. The steam billowed out, warm and inviting, and I could just make out Cerys's silhouette through the plastic curtain.

Before I could locate some sense, I swept the curtain aside and stepped into the bathtub. The warm steam engulfed my body, but I barely felt it.

I tried to keep my eyes off Cerys. I really did.

But it was like telling a drumbeat not to echo. Impossible.

She stood under the stream, water flowing over her curves, rivulets tracing paths I longed to follow with my tongue. Her eyes were closed, dark lashes fanning against her cheeks as she tilted her head back, letting the water soak her hair. I couldn't look away.

"You gonna stand there all day, or are you actually going to wash up?" Cerys asked, her voice barely audible over the sound of the water. Her eyes fluttered open, catching me staring. I quickly looked away, expecting a sharp rebuke.

"Sorry, I..." I started, but she cut me off with a soft snort.

"Was just admiring the view?"

"Maybe?" I reached for the soap, needing to do something, anything, to distract myself from the way her body called to mine.

She snorted, turning around to face the flow of water, giving me a full view of her back and biteable ass. "Well, admire while you wash. We don't have all day."

"You're not going to tell me off for it?" I asked cautiously.

"Would you prefer I did?"

I shook my head, confusion swirling in my mind. "No, it's just... unexpected. A few hours ago, you could barely stand to look at me."

Cerys shrugged, turning back to the water. "I'm tired of fighting."

Frowning, I lathered up, trying to focus on the mundane task of cleaning myself. But my gaze kept drifting back to Cerys, to the way her hands glided over her skin, the way the soap suds traced paths down her arms. I was painfully hard, my cock aching with every beat of my heart.

This is a terrible idea. I should get out. Use the other bathroom.

But my feet stayed rooted to the spot, my body yearning for something it had wanted for years.

"Could you..." Her words trailed off as she turned to face me. "Could you wash my back?"

I hesitated before nodding. My hands trembled as I accepted the soap from her. Jaw tight, I worked the bar into a lather, trying to steady my nerves. She turned back around, giving me space, but a part of me felt frozen in place, I couldn't make myself reach out.

Which was laughable really. The guy who drummed in front of thousands, was fumbling over washing a woman's back. But this wasn't just any woman.

Cerys, impatient as ever, snapped over her shoulder, "What are you waiting for, Nick? A written invitation?"

The tension between us shifted, turning familiar in a way that was both comforting and unsettling. This was familiar territory, the kind we'd perfected over years of friendship and silent longing.

I focused on the soap, its slippery texture under my fingers a welcome distraction from the racket of worries and fears inside my head. The warmth of the water, the scent of the soap, the quiet intimacy of the moment — it was all so overwhelming, yet so right.

I started at her shoulders, gently massaging the suds into her skin. I worked my way down, tracing the curve of her back, taking more pleasure than I should have in the way her muscles tensed and relaxed under my touch.

When I finished, I was breathless, and my cock ached with a need that was almost painful. I rinsed the soap from my hands, trying to ignore the throbbing pulse of desire that coursed through me.

Cerys turned back around. Her darkened eyes locked onto mine. "Your turn," she whispered, her voice hoarse, making me question if she felt the impact as deeply as I did.

"Okay." I barely got the word out, my voice thick with need.

We shuffled awkwardly, trying to swap places in the small space. I attempted to avoid touching her again, but there really wasn't room. A jolt ran through me as my cock grazed her stomach, and we both froze. That small brush sent a jolt of pleasure through me, and I bit my cheek hard to snuff out the groan building at the back of my throat.

Cerys's pupils dilated, her lips parting as she drew in a shaky breath. Every reason this was a bad idea flooded my mind, but I couldn't focus on any of them. Not with her so close. She chewed on her lower lip, drawing my gaze, and making me wonder if she was as affected as I was.

The air between us crackled with tension, the quiet pressing in from all sides.

I couldn't say who moved first. All I knew was that one moment we were standing there, frozen like statues, and the next, my lips were on hers, hungry and demanding. She responded in kind, her arms wrapping around my neck, pulling me closer.

I picked her up, her legs wrapping around my waist, and pressed her against the wall. My cock grazed her pussy, and we both groaned, the sound echoing in the small space. Years of denied need surged through me, drowning out any rational thought. All that mattered was Cerys, her mouth hot and demanding, her tongue delving past my lips to claim me. The world narrowed to the press of her body, the taste of her, the desperate need to make her mine.

CHAPTER EIGHT

CERYS

This was a bad idea.

As soon as the floodwater cleared, he'd be gone. There were no ifs or buts about it.

Nick Davies never stuck around. Not eight years ago, and certainly not now. So why was I opening myself up to hurt? Letting old feelings and a few shared laughs cloud my judgement, knowing he had and always would choose his music career over anything — or anyone — else.

Of all the people to rebound on, did you have to pick him?

Was it a rebound if I'd been tragically single for eight years?

Even so, guilt twisted in my gut.

Yet I couldn't tear my lips from his. All my reservations began to melt like cheese on hot toast. My fingers threaded through his damp hair, pulling him closer, deepening the kiss. His mouth was hot and insistent, his tongue exploring mine with an intensity that left me breathless.

Maybe it was the adrenaline from the day's unexpected turn, or the intimacy of being stranded together, but everything about this moment felt both inevitable and terrifying. I wanted him — had always wanted him, if I was honest with myself. But could I handle the fallout when he left again?

Nick trailed kisses along my jaw and down my neck, nibbling and licking the water from my skin. My head lolled back against the tiled wall, a sigh escaping me.

I should stop this.

But then he dragged his lips down my neck, pinning me to the wall with his body. All coherent thought melted away.

His breath was hot as he nipped at the

curve where my neck met my shoulder. It set off a cascade of goosebumps, each one tingling like the first rush of cold air on a winter morning. Hands roamed over me, tracing the curves of my breasts. He cupped them gently, his thumbs brushing over my nipples, sending jolts of pleasure straight to my core. I arched into his touch, my body craving more.

But he took his time, his touch reverent, almost worshipful while the calluses on his fingertips added a layer of roughness to his gentle caress.

I rocked my hips, seeking friction, enjoying the way his hardness slid against my clit. Waves of pleasure radiated from that point of contact, sending heat spiralling through my veins. His mouth found my breast, his tongue and lips teasing my nipple, sucking and licking until I was a writhing mess of need, drawing out a gasp from deep within me. He repeated the action with the other breast, driving me wild.

Nick reclaimed my lips in a slow, drugging kiss, while his hands slid down to my thighs, then back up to my waist, his fingers digging into my flesh with a possessive grip. Every part of him was taut and ready.

His hands gripped my ass, cupping it firmly, pulling me even closer, heightening the tiny bursts of friction that were driving me mad with desperation.

I was lost in the sensation, lost in him. The world outside faded away, leaving only the two of us, our bodies pressed together, our breaths mingling, our hearts beating in sync.

The first flicker of an orgasm fluttered inside of me and I moaned. I ground against him harder, chasing the release I so desperately needed. His hand slipped between us, his fingers finding my clit with unerring accuracy. He rubbed slow circles, applying just the right amount of pressure to send me spiralling over the edge.

I cried out, clinging to him as waves of pleasure crashed over me. He stilled, his forehead resting against mine, his breath ragged and hot on my face.

"Cerys," Nick rasped, his voice rough with desire and emotion. "Are you sure you want to keep going?"

No. Yes. Maybe.

"If you stop now, I'll turn all your drumsticks into firewood and make you play with cheese wheels instead!" I blurted out, my cheeks flushing as I realised how ridiculous and desperate I sounded.

Nick burst out laughing, his eyes crinkling at the corners. "That's a new one."

His amusement was infectious, and I found myself grinning back at him.

"But I'm serious. I need you to fuck me. Right now." My eyes narrowed at the note of desperation in my tone.

If I could convince him — and myself — that this was just a fleeting moment, maybe I could watch him leave without shattering completely. Self-preservation was a fine art, and right now, I was Vermeer.

"But this doesn't change anything. When we get out of this shower, I still won't..."

Nick circled his thumb around my nipple, smirking as my words trailed off into a moan.

"You seem to like me just fine right now."

Oh, who was I kidding? The chances

of getting out of this unscathed were about as slim as finding a unicorn in the Welsh countryside.

"Just fuck me already."

Nick's eyes darkened with desire and something deeper. He adjusted our position, lining himself up at my entrance. His hard cock pressed against me. But he paused, and for a moment, I panicked, thinking he'd changed his mind.

"I don't have a condom," he said, his voice strained. "I'm clean, but—"

"I'm on the pill. Just get inside me."

With a groan, he slid into me, filling me completely. I gasped at the sensation, my body stretching to accommodate him. It had been so long — too long — since I'd been filled at all.

"Fuck, you feel incredible," Nick growled, his eyes locked onto mine. "So tight, so perfect."

He quickly made me realise the problem had been the men I'd picked since Gareth. The way he pumped into me, grazing my clit with each thrust, holding me up without even looking strained — it was like nothing I'd ever experienced.

"God, Nick," I moaned, my nails digging into his shoulders. "That's... you're..."

My eyelids fluttered as he thrust into me again.

"I'm what, Cerys?" he asked, his voice rough as he drove deeper. "Tell me."

"Exquisite. Perfect," I breathed, my eyes flickering shut.

He might have ruined me for sex with anyone else after this. My vibrators might not be enough. And the strangest part? I wasn't even upset about it.

His fingers dug into my hips, holding me steady as he drove into me, his gaze locked onto mine, intense and unyielding. I clung to him, my nails raking down his back, marking him as he marked me. Each thrust muddied my thoughts, making me forget momentarily why something that felt so incredible could be a bad idea.

The steam from the shower enveloped us, creating a cocoon of heat and sensation that blocked out the rest of the world.

Right now, all I cared about was the way his cock owned me and the pressure building deep within me, begging for release.

Nick's mouth found mine again, his kiss hungry and demanding. Our tongues clashed as I matched him with my own demands. I could almost taste his hunger. I met each of his thrusts with a roll of my hips, taking him deeper, urging him on.

"Fuck, Cerys," Nick groaned, tearing his mouth from mine to bury his face in my neck. His breath was hot and ragged, his voice a low growl. "You're so fucking tight, strangling my cock like a good girl."

A shiver ran through me at his words, my pussy clenching around him. Nick grunted in response, his voice rough with pleasure. "That's it, squeeze me just like that, babe."

I could only respond with a moan, my body too consumed with sensation to form coherent words. My fingers tangled in his hair, holding him close as he ravaged my neck, his teeth grazing my skin. Each thrust of his hips sent waves of pleasure crashing through me, building and building until I was a writhing, gasping mess.

"Nick," I breathed, my voice hitching as he hit a spot deep inside me that made stars explode behind my eyelids. His name was a plea, a prayer, and a curse all rolled into one. I was so close, teetering on the edge of something monumental, something that threatened to shatter me into a million pieces and force me to see him in a new light.

He adjusted his angle, hitting that spot again and again, driving me closer to the edge with each thrust.

"Come on," he growled, his voice rough and commanding. "Let go. Come for me."

His hand snaked between us, his fingers finding my clit and circling it. The combination of his cock filling me and his fingers working their magic was more than I could handle. I was a live wire, sparking and crackling, ready to explode.

"I... I can't..." I gasped, my body tensing as I teetered on the brink.

"Yes, you can. Let go, Cerys. I've got you."

Why would I trust him now, when he had a track record of letting me down when I needed him most?

Yet, my body betrayed my doubts, responding to his touch. His fingers moved faster, applying just the right pressure, sending me spiralling out of control. I cried out, my pussy convulsing around him, my vision blurring with the force of my climax. Nick followed me over the edge, his body stiffening as he found his own release. He groaned my name, his face buried in my neck, his arms holding me tight.

"You might not like me," he murmured. "But your body sure as hell does."

I hummed in response. Incapable of thinking straight or stringing together a sensible reply that wouldn't come back to bite me.

I let my head fall back against the tile, savouring how my body still hummed from... well, that. Every nerve tingled, aftershocks rippling through me.

My mind was a disaster zone, however. Half of it wanted to put my leftover cheese wax to work building a replica of his cock.

Just for, you know, scientific purposes. The other half was plagued with more feelings than it knew how to handle. The walls I'd built over the years were crumbling faster than a poorly aged Caerphilly, and I didn't stand a chance.

How could being with him feel so right and so utterly wrong at the same time? The anger I'd clung to like a lifeline was slipping away, my resentment melting.

I squeezed my eyes shut, trying to shove down the emotional tidal wave threatening to drown me. Flashes of the past flickered behind my eyelids — Nick standing up to that bully in Year 10, even though he was a gangly beanpole back then. Spending a whole Saturday helping me fix Dad's old tractor, just to dodge Mam's nagging. We had our own language — eye rolls and snarky comments that said more than any heart-to-heart ever could. Now it felt as distant as that elusive family cheese recipe I still couldn't crack.

Then Gareth died, and everything shattered. The gut-wrenching emptiness swallowed me whole. I'd been angry at him for leaving me. For not being there to hold me when the world fell apart. For not sharing in the grief that had consumed me. I'd blamed him for everything — ditching Gareth's memory, chasing his rock star life while we were stuck here.

Now the truth slammed into me.

It had never been about Gareth.

He'd left *me*.

All of these years, I'd been nursing the pain of my best friend — the man I thought I could always rely on — abandoning me, too. And admitting that felt like ripping open an old wound.

CHAPTER NINE

NICK

I stepped out of the shower, avoiding Cerys's gaze. The cool air hit my damp skin like a slap of reality. What the fuck had I done?

Steam curled around us, dissipating along with the heat of passion and the scent of sex, leaving...what, exactly? Guilt? Regret? The bitter taste of betrayal?

"You okay?" Cerys brushed past me, reaching for a towel. Even that brief contact sent electricity through me.

"Fine."

She raised a brow, clearly unconvinced. But she didn't push, focusing instead on wrapping the towel around herself. I grabbed mine, scrubbing it over my skin with more force than necessary, trying to ground myself in the coarse texture rather than the memory of her lips.

"Looks like we both need a fresh set of clothes," I said, trying to keep my tone light despite the guilt eating me alive.

Cerys nodded, adjusting her towel. "I keep spares for when cheesemaking gets messy. You, on the other hand…" She paused, a wry glint in her eyes as she raked them over me. "Well, you can borrow some of Gareth's old things. Unless you'd prefer to stay naked, which for the record, I have no issue with at all."

I forced a laugh, though it felt hollow. Wearing Gareth's clothes made my skin crawl.

"I'll, uh, go see what I can find."

She scooped up the dirty clothes, and we shuffled awkwardly into the hallway. I turned towards the stairs and Gareth's room, while Cerys headed for the kitchen.

"Nick." Her voice was soft, hesitant.

I paused, but didn't turn. I couldn't face her. It was too much. I had to get out of there, had to escape the suffocating weight of my own shame.

"I don't regret it."

My eyes squeezed shut. A part of me soared at her confession, while another part recoiled in disbelief. How could she not?

She hated me. This had to be some cruel joke or a moment of confused feelings. I couldn't let myself believe otherwise.

I fled upstairs without answering, like the coward she accused me of being. My pace slowed when I reached Gareth's old bedroom door. Eight years had passed since I'd last stood in that room, but I knew what I'd find inside. A shrine. Well, not in the literal sense. But the room had been frozen in time.

Meinir never had the heart to clear it out. Each time I suggested it, her eyes filled with tears, and I apologised, dropping the subject.

I braced myself, then pushed it open. If only it had squeaked, giving me some warning, some reason to hesitate. I hovered in the doorway, my gaze sweeping over the familiar space.

His band posters still papered the walls. The guitar his dad had bought him from the pawn shop was propped in the corner. Even his bed was unmade, though Meins had picked up all his dirty clothes that once littered the floor.

My chest ached and my feet refused to move, to spoil the snapshot of time by rifling through his drawers.

But the alternative was far worse.

So I gave in and rushed in, my gaze fixed on the dresser like tunnel vision would hold the memories at bay. My hands shook as I yanked open the dresser drawer, desperate for something to cover up my shame. I sifted through the options, catching very faint whiffs of Gareth's aftershave as I disturbed the forgotten fabric. It hit me like a punch to the gut.

Each shirt, each pair of jeans, carried memories of a time when we were inseparable. A time before guilt and regret became my constant companions.

I pulled out the first faded T-shirt my

fingers settled on. My heart lurched at the sight of the stupid slogan — I'm with the band — the one he'd worn on his first date with Cerys. She'd laughed so hard when she saw it, she'd snorted. I'd had to listen to her gush about how adorable and funny he was for weeks after.

I dropped the T-shirt. No way could I wear that shirt after I'd just...

Christ. What kind of friend was I?

I swallowed hard against the bile rising in my throat and I grabbed a pair of jeans and a plain, nondescript T-shirt and bolted from the room.

Funny how karma works, isn't it? I'd spent years running from this place, from the memories, from the guilt. Now I was literally trapped by a flood, forced to face everything I'd been avoiding.

And what did I do?

I slept with my dead best friend's girl.

Fucking brilliant, Nick. Real stellar work there, mate.

As I slipped the clothes on, I couldn't escape the truth. I'd betrayed my best friend, even if he was no longer here to see it.

The hallway mirror reflected a stranger — a man wearing another man's clothes, another man's life. I turned away, unable to face the accusation in my own eyes. I needed to get out of this house, away from these ghosts.

I trudged back downstairs and glanced out of the window, stupid hope taking root in my chest. The downpour hadn't stopped, which meant I had to go into the kitchen and pretend nothing had happened. That she hadn't blown my mind and given me a glimpse of a dream I'd long ago buried.

"Did you find something?" Cerys asked when I stepped into the kitchen. She stood at the counter, pouring steaming water into mugs.

"Yeah." I tugged at the collar. "Though the faster my clothes dry the happier I'll be."

She glanced over her shoulder and chuckled at the sight of my pained expression. I pulled out a chair and sank into it, glaring at her all the while.

"They're just clothes."

I grunted in acknowledgement. Yes,

they were just clothes. But they were the second thing of his I'd taken in less than an hour.

"What do you want to do during our captivity?" Cerys placed a steaming mug of builder's tea on the table in front of me. "No sugar. Splash of milk. Brewed until you could stand a spoon up in it."

She took a seat while I stared at it, even more perplexed. She remembered how I took my tea?

This sudden shift in her demeanour threw me for a loop.

She chattered away, her tone light and friendly. I nodded along, munching on a biscuit, struggling to keep up with this bizarre turn of events.

"I can't believe I slept with my best friend's girl," I muttered to myself. "What the hell is wrong with me?"

"Excuse me?" Cerys's mug clattered against the table, her eyes narrowing. "Is that all I am to you? Just 'your best friend's girl'?"

I winced. "No, I didn't mean—"

"Oh, spare me," she snapped. "Men

are all the same — reducing women to possessions, like we don't get a say."

"You're twisting my words." I tried to keep calm, but her fury tore through me.

She leaned forward, eyes blazing. "Am I? Or are you more worried about some 'bro code' than the fact we just shared something meaningful?"

I sighed, running a hand through my damp hair. "I can't shake the feeling I betrayed him. Gareth deserved better."

"Gareth is dead," Cerys said, her voice cold. "And we're still here."

The blunt statement crushed the air from my lungs, leaving me stunned and breathless. I knew he was gone. How could I ever forget?

Still I stumbled back, needing something solid to hold on to, and sank into a kitchen chair. My elbows dug into the table as I buried my face in my hands. A familiar, gnawing guilt clawed at my insides, threatening to swallow me whole.

She didn't get it. How could she? I'd never told her, or anyone for that matter, that I blamed myself.

I should have been there. If I'd been

home, if I'd gone with him that night, maybe things would have been different. Maybe Gareth would still be here, laughing, living, making plans with Cerys. Instead, I was the one left standing.

I rubbed my temples, trying to push back the tide of regret that threatened to pull me under. Survivor's guilt, my therapist called it. But it felt more like a life sentence.

"Yeah." I forced out a whisper, each word scraping my throat. "And whose fault is that?"

I gestured wildly at the photo. "He deserved better than me for a best friend."

"Don't make this all about you." Cerys rose, her expression hardening.

I spun, fists clenched at my sides. "What do you want? An apology? I'm sorry, okay? I'm sorry I wasn't there that night. I'm sorry I couldn't save him. I'm sorry I'm such a screw up that I slept with my dead best friend's girlfriend!"

Silence fell, heavy as a stone. Cerys just looked at me, her disappointment flickering beneath the anger.

"You want to know what I really blame you for?" she asked softly.

My heart pounded. *Here it comes.* "What?"

Her answer gutted me. "You left," she said, each word hitting me like a punch to the gut. "I needed you, and you left."

CERYS

Nick looked as if I'd slapped him. That raw, startled expression was so unlike his usual bravado that I nearly apologised on the spot. But I couldn't take a single syllable back.

His mouth worked, but no sound came out.

He swallowed hard, guilt etched into the lines around his eyes. "I couldn't come back. The band needed me."

"And I didn't?" My voice wobbled despite my best efforts. "Or do I not count, since I can't pack a concert venue?"

He ran a hand over his hair, still damp

from the shower we shouldn't have shared but did. "I thought you didn't—" He exhaled, a tremor catching in his throat. "I was sure you hated me."

My grip on the table tightened. "Maybe I did. But not because of Gareth's accident."

His eyes flickered with uncertainty. "Then why?"

I glared at him, but what else was I meant to say? I wanted him — no, I needed him — to listen to me.

We couldn't move on unless he did, and I really wanted to fucking move on.

I leaned forward, heart pounding. "You were supposed to be my friend too, not just Gareth's. When I needed you most, you *vanished*."

His eyes clouded with guilt. "I—"

"Was I prickly with you?" I pressed on, cutting him off.

He shook his head.

"Did I scream at you or tell you never to call me again?"

"No."

"Then where the fuck did you get the idea that I hated you, Nick?"

Nick dragged a chair back and sank onto it, the dull scrape echoing in the kitchen. "I've spent eight years blaming myself for Gareth's death. If I'd been home that night, if I'd driven him—" His voice broke.

A shock tore through my system. All this time, he'd been shouldering that guilt? My throat tightened, but I refused to let sympathy crowd out my anger.

"I was sure you thought the same." Nick's breathing turned ragged. "I thought staying away would spare you more pain. I... told myself you didn't want me screwing up your life any more than I already had."

"So you decided for me that I'd never want to see you again? Brilliant. I was already grieving one person. You made me grieve two." Unshed tears burned in my eyes, but I refused to cry in front of him again. "I hated you for running away. Not for Gareth's accident."

He flinched. "I didn't know."

"No," I muttered, "you didn't bother finding out. Not even when my dad died." The old hurt rose up, raw and choking.

He opened his mouth, but no words came. His stare dropped to the tabletop as though it held answers. "When I did try, you told me to get lost."

I grimaced, recalling that day — up to my elbows in uncooperative curds, exhausted and in no mood for his cameo appearance. "You popped in for all of ninety seconds. I was furious because you acted like you could waltz in, ask how I was, then dash off again."

His breath hitched. "You told me to go back to my stage."

"No. I told you to fuck off and stick your drumsticks up your ass." My cheeks heated with shame.

A flash of sorrow crossed his face. "I drove home thinking that was it — that I'd do more harm than good if I tried again."

My heart twisted. "Maybe I wouldn't have been so harsh if you'd sent so much as a text before two years had passed."

He nodded miserably. "I'm not arguing. I messed up every way possible. The band needed me and I leaned into it."

A lump formed in my throat. A tear

slipped down my cheek. I let it fall. "I needed you, and you were gone."

His head snapped up, tears gathering in the corners of his eyes. "I've hurt you so badly. I never wanted that."

"Funny how intentions don't match outcomes." I pressed trembling fingers to my temple. "Why did you even come back?"

"I couldn't stay away forever. Meinir deserved some time, and I—" He pressed his lips together, seeming to brace himself. "And I guess part of me hoped I"d run into you. To see if you could ever forgive me."

I considered him, every one of my old scars throbbing. My breath caught. "Do you have any idea how often I wished you'd walk through that door? I mean af-ter..." I pinched the bridge of my nose, frustration pulsing through me.

Would it have been different if I'd put on a polite expression the day he'd dropped in? Probably. But it wouldn't have changed the pain he'd caused me.

"Why didn't you call?" My voice trem-bled with pain. "You still haven't answered that properly. Were you scared you'd hear me cry? Scared I'd tear into you?"

Nick inhaled sharply. "Yes. At least I could control the script in my head. If I heard your voice, it'd confirm every awful thing I already believed." He grimaced. "And then I dodged you whenever I came home. Too afraid I'd see your eyes and know exactly how badly I failed."

I brushed the back of my hand across my cheek, collecting another errant tear. The overhead light flickered briefly. We both glanced up, but it held steady.

"You truly believed I'd hold you responsible for Gareth?"

"Why not? I blamed me." His blue eyes glistened. "Every single day. Still do, if I'm honest. If I'd been there, if I'd driven, if I'd stopped him — maybe he'd still be alive. Maybe you wouldn't look at me like I'm a traitor."

The storm hissed against the window, reminding me how precarious our situation was — both physically and emotionally. My anger warred with the surge of pity that threatened to soften me. I fought it back.

"Stop saying things like that. It wasn't your fault."

"I know. But if I'd been there, he'd still be alive."

He blew out a breath and shook his head. Tears clung to his lashes, making my heart twist in sympathy.

Thunder rattled the kitchen again. His eyes flickered with something I couldn't read, like regret and longing twisted together. My heart hammered, half expecting him to spout some excuse about how he'd never meant to hurt me. But he only stared, chest heaving.

Nick swallowed hard, throat bobbing. "I know I can't erase what I did, and I'm truly sorry for all the pain I caused you, but tell me how to fix this and I'll do it. Anything."

My mind flashed to the way he'd pinned me in the shower, the swirl of lust and guilt that followed. I swallowed, gripping the chair so tightly it hurt.

"We can't just pop open some magic kit and rebuild the last eight years. We move forward, or we don't."

"Forward how? You said you hated me—"

"Jesus, do you never listen?" Frustration coated my words. "I hated that you could chase your dream and leave me stuck in the same town, burying the dead. I hated missing you so much it hurt."

"I missed you every day." Nick stood, crossing the kitchen in two strides, stopping just short of touching me. "When I finished a show, I'd wish you were there. Then I'd remember what I'd done. And I'd drink a little too much or find another distraction."

I stared up at him, my heart in my throat. "So you want to keep drowning your regrets?"

"No," he whispered. "I want—" He hesitated, gaze drifting to my mouth, the tension between us crackling. He stared at me with a helpless expression.

"I want you," I said, forcing down the buzz of fear that he'd reject me. "Not as a friend. Not as a guilt-ridden ghost trying to compete with Gareth's memory. *You*, Nick. I want you to stay because you want *me*, too. And if you can't admit that, you can walk out that door when it's all clear."

He inhaled sharply, gaze flicking to the windows where the rain beat a relentless tattoo. "Cerys…"

"Don't 'Cerys' me and then shut down. You said you want to fix things — so do it. Stop fidgeting like you're ready to bolt."

His hand curled at his side, knuckles whitening. "It's not that simple."

"Make it simple."

"You don't—" He pinched the bridge of his nose and groaned. "If I agree to that do, it'll feel like I'm betraying Gareth, like I'm—"

"Stealing his girl?" My voice shook with anger. "He's dead, Nick. We didn't have a crystal ball. If he'd lived, maybe we'd have broken up. Maybe not. But you're still here, and I'm still here, so who the hell decided you have no right to me?"

He winced. "He was my best friend."

"I know." The lump in my throat thickened. "But you're trying to use a dead man's memory to run my life. I'm done with it. I'm done letting your guilt dictate my choices.

I've loved you — God, probably since I was a teenager." A tear spilled down my cheek, but I ploughed on, refusing to let him slip away into another excuse. "You love your band. Good. I'm not asking you to quit. But if you're going to flee the second a gig is scheduled, don't tell me it's because you're 'protecting' me. Own it: you're scared to love me because you think Gareth's ghost will pummel you in your sleep."

Nick's cheeks flushed, shame and yearning flickering in his eyes. "I am scared," he whispered. "I keep seeing his face whenever I think of you—"

"Well, I see his face every time I look at you." Tears burned my eyes, spilling over at last. "Doesn't mean I'm not ready to live again. You think I never questioned my own feelings?" My voice cracked, but I straightened my shoulders. "I'm done questioning. I'm telling you now: I want to move on, *with* you, because I love you more than I can stand. If you can't handle it, go. I won't beg."

He clenched his jaw, tears pooling in his eyes. His mouth opened, but words didn't come. Instead, he stepped closer, close enough that all I had to do was sway and I'd brush against him.

"Cerys…" He reached a trembling hand up to cup my cheek. "I've been in love with you since we were kids. Since that stupid sack race where you tripped and made us lose, and I didn't care because you smiled at me like I'd hang your whole world."

He actually said it. Effervescent bubbles exploded in my stomach. "You loved me even then?"

He smiled, shaking a little with a strangled laugh.

"How could I not? I thought I was just being loyal to Gareth, giving him the first shot. But after he… it felt like the worst betrayal possible to want you. So I stayed away."

I narrowed my eyes on him and covered his hand with mine. "That's the problem: you decided for me. You never asked how I felt. Guess what? I've wanted you too, you colossal idiot."

"God," he breathed, voice a reverent

hush. "You have no idea how often I've dreamt of hearing that."

I curled my fingers into his shirt. "Then hear it again. I. Want. You. Not a once-off in the shower, not a pity fling. I want you in every messy, complicated way." I swallowed a sob. "I can't keep living in this half-life where I pretend I don't care that you're gone. I won't."

Lightning streaked across the sky, illuminating every conflicting emotion on his face.

"I can't tell you the guilt will vanish overnight. It won't. But Gareth…" I swallowed hard, my throat tightening. "Gareth loved you. You were his brother in every way that mattered. And if he could say anything right now, he'd tell you to stop torturing yourself. He'd tell you it's okay to be happy. To be with me if that's what makes us happy."

Nick exhaled, his breath trembling against my palms. "I can't just flick a switch and stop feeling like I failed him."

"I know." My voice cracked. "But you didn't fail him by loving me."

He blinked hard. "Cerys—"

"Don't," I whispered. "Don't say my name like that and then back away again. If you truly believe Gareth would hate you for loving me, you're wrong. And if you're just afraid, admit it and let's fight that fear together. But don't pretend this is about loyalty to him. It's about you thinking you don't deserve happiness."

He closed his eyes. "I can't walk away from you. Not anymore."

A shiver tore through me. "Prove it. Don't blame the band, or me, or Gareth. Own that you want me and that you'll stay."

He dragged in a shaky breath, his hand hovering near mine. "I've wanted you for so long, I don't remember not wanting you."

My heart lurched, tears prickling again. "Then be brave enough to say yes."

Nick's hands fell to my waist and he pulled me flush against him. "Yes."

I grabbed his collar, yanking him into a kiss that was raw, desperate — laden with every moment we'd lost. The world vanished, replaced by the slide of his lips and the thunder of my pulse. We clung to each other, each groan and gasp pulling us deeper. The warmth of his chest, and the faint scent of my shampoo on his skin all collided in a dizzying rush. I pressed myself closer, fisting the fabric of Gareth's old T-shirt at his shoulders, the irony not lost on me. But Nick's warmth and the trembling press of his lips wiped every thought clean except for him.

CHAPTER ELEVEN

NICK

"Warm enough?" I tugged Cerys closer under the thick wool blanket. A fire burned in the hearth and the candles she'd scavenged from random drawers flickered around us.

This was the kind of moment I'd always dreamed of but never thought I'd actually get. Holding her in my arms, feeling her breath on my neck, watching the firelight dance in her eyes. It didn't seem real. How many years had I spent wishing for this? How many times had I told myself I didn't deserve it?

She nestled against my side, her palm resting on my chest. "I'm not shivering, if that's what you're asking." A corner of her mouth quirked.

"Could've fooled me," I said, keeping my voice low.

"You're the one who insisted on bundling me up like a burrito."

A smile tugged at my lips. "In fairness, a blanket and a burrito aren't that different. Both keep you warm."

She let out a quiet laugh, and the tension I'd been carrying slipped away. We'd clashed and argued so much — this felt almost unreal.

Tracing lazy circles on my chest, she tilted her head back until her amused gaze clashed with mine. "Do you think Meinir planned all this?"

I snorted. "I'll admit, she's capable of miracles." She got us both in the house at the same time after all. "But weather manipulation might be a step too far — even for her."

"Oh, I don't know." She smirked. "If anyone could, it'd be her. If she can convince the entire village that the cider festival was rescheduled, just to win the pie contest, she can do anything."

"That was different." That was strategic genius. "This would require divine powers."

"You know better than to underestimate Meins," Cerys said, amusement tingeing her serious tone. "She's probably out there now, summoning a second flood to keep you here longer."

I squeezed her against my side. "Wouldn't mind being stranded with you a bit longer."

"Careful." She bit her lip, batting her lashes at me. "You'll make me think you like me."

Her words settled like a well-placed chess move, deliberate and daring, waiting for my next play. Her lashes swept low, framing eyes that sparkled in the firelight. God, she was something else.

"I wouldn't want to ruin the suspense, but if you're still guessing, I must be doing something wrong."

She tapped her fingers against my

chest, her touch light and rhythmic. "You've got that rock star confidence down to a science, don't you?"

"Gotta keep the fans guessing."

Her fingers stilled and something shifted in her expression — like she was really seeing me for the first time, not as the boy who left, but as the man who'd come back.

"You really could, couldn't you?"

"Could what?" The teasing note slipped from my voice as a furrow creased her brow.

I searched her face and she shook her head, like she wasn't sure she wanted to say it out loud.

"Have anyone. Any life. Anywhere. You could pick... anything."

I slid my hand up to cup her face, brushing my thumb along her cheekbone. "I did pick. And I'm right where I want to be."

Her lips parted as if to respond, but no words came. For once, Cerys Evans was speechless, and I savoured every second of it.

I'd never associated silence with Cerys

before, and it hit me like a rare gift. I couldn't stop myself from leaning in, brushing the faintest kiss against her forehead. It wasn't enough — nothing ever would be — but it felt like the right place to start. A small promise for everything I still owed her.

She blinked up at me, a flicker of doubt crossed her face. "You live in Cardiff," she said, her words measured, testing. "Your band's taking off. You'll be on the road... a lot."

She didn't flinch, but the edge in her voice told me she was bracing for something. Like the distance was already pulling us apart, even while she sat in my arms.

"Babe, that's not even a competition." I shifted onto my side and pulled her down beside me, wrapping my arm around her waist.

I didn't believe she'd run away from me, not now — and how ironic would it be if she turned the tables on me now that I'd admitted the truth. Even so, a little caution never hurt anyone. She bit her lip, her teeth catching at the soft skin in a way that sent my heart racing. It was strange, seeing her unsure. Cerys had always been fire and certainty — all sharp edges and bravery.

My fingers traced slow soothing circles on her hip while I pressed my forehead against hers. "I need the band. It's my heartbeat. But you're the rest of me. Eight years without you, and I've never felt as whole as I do holding you now."

Her eyes widened. "Nick—"

"I mean it," I said, my voice firm, but gentle. "Cilwen, Cardiff, London — hell, I'd set up a practice space in your cheese cave if it meant being close to you."

That earned me a faint laugh. "You'd last a day."

Her fingers brushed along my wrist, steady and soft. Something low and electric stirred deep inside me, like the first note of a song I'd been desperate to hear. I swallowed hard.

"I'd make it two."

She smirked, that maddening little quirk of her lips that always seemed to carry its own brand of defiance. "Oh, I'd pay to see it. You and a wheel of Gouda, side by side. The headline writes itself: Rockstar Turned Cheese Curd Wrangler."

The way she relaxed into my arms made everything else — every fear, every regret — melt away.

"Don't tempt me," I said, my tone lighter now. "I bet the acoustics are perfect there."

She laughed, and my chest ached. My pulse kicked up, my grip instinctively tightening around her like I needed that sound to stay with me.

"Oh, I'm sure you'd turn it into your personal studio in no time."

"But seriously." I framed her face with my hands, holding her gaze steady. "I meant what I said in the kitchen. The band means everything to me, but I want you to be my world. I'll make it work. Move here, figure it out — whatever it takes. I'm not losing this chance."

Her fingers froze mid-pattern on my chest, her green eyes searching mine. "You'd really give up everything?"

"Not everything," I said, my voice soft but firm. "Music is as necessary to me as breathing. But I'd give up any version of my life that didn't have you in it. You said you loved me. I'm holding you to that."

She blinked, her lips parting as if to argue, but the words never came. Instead, she leaned into me, her forehead brushing my neck. "When do you leave?" she whispered.

"In two weeks."

She winced. "That's so soon."

"It is." I nodded, sliding my hand beneath the blanket. "But it's enough time to sort a few things out."

"Like what?"

"Like convincing you to meet me on tour." The need for her to say yes burned through me with a foreign desperation. She'd had a one-track mind in school though, and based on Meins's comments earlier today, she hadn't changed. I needed to pull out every trick I had, every card I could play. Starting with the slow, teasing circles my fingers traced on her hip, each one designed to unravel her resolve. "We're playing Rome. You've always wanted to go. Why not now?"

Her lashes lowered, her eyes darkening as her focus drifted down. A faint shiver ran through her before my words seemed to click. Her gaze snapped back to mine, surprise flickering across her face.

"You're serious?"

"Of course I am." I smiled. Shocked awe looked good on her. My hand slid to her ass, fingers spread wide. "It's just two weeks. You can handle that."

She chewed her lip. "I don't know..."

"What's there to know? I'm not asking you to put your life on hold for six months and move into the tour bus. Though, I wouldn't be opposed." I gripped her ass, pulling her firmly against me, ensuring she could feel just how much the idea appealed to me.

Her eyes narrowed, her hand bracing against my chest, but her lips twitched. "A tour bus with you lot? That's not living the dream, Nick. That's suffering."

I raised a brow while my hands skimmed back up to her waist and my fingertips teased the bare skin just above her leggings. "You've never even seen the bus."

"Don't need to. I can smell the bad decisions from here." Her mock-serious expression slackened as my hand slipped up her T-shirt, skimming along her waist.

My thumb grazed the underside of her breast, and her lips parted.

"Fair," I said, unable to hide my smile. "But think of the perks. Private shows. Backstage passes. Room service if you ask nicely."

Her breath caught as my fingers traced higher, my palm cupping the soft swell of her breast. "Room service?" She arched into my touch. "In a bus?"

"Fine, less room service, more take-away bags and questionable catering. But the private shows are a guarantee." I teased her nipple with my thumb. A soft moan escaped her lips as the sensitive bud peaked. "Name the song, and I'll play it for you."

"Bit desperate, aren't you?" Her hand stilled on my chest, her nails digging into my skin through my shirt. "Using bribes now?"

"Whatever it takes." I let my mouth drift to her neck, my teeth grazing her pulse point while my hand traced a path back to her waist. "I'm not above begging, either."

Her laugh was low, but I caught the

way her breath stuttered when my hand slipped beneath her waistband. "You? Beg? I'd pay to see it."

She rolled her hips, grinding against me, and I groaned low in my throat.

"Careful." I kissed the spot just beneath her ear, my tongue flicking out to taste her skin. "That's an offer I'll hold you to."

Her hand clenched in my shirt, her back arching as she pressed closer. "And what happens after Rome? You're back on the road. I'm here alone."

"I'm not leaving you behind again." I cupped her face, brushing my thumb along her cheek. "This isn't some temporary thing. I'm moving home. I'll be in Cardiff when I need to practice, I'll tour when I have to, but the rest of the time, I'm here. With you."

Her brows knitted, her lips parting slightly. "You'd really do that?"

"I already decided," I said, my voice steady. "This is where I want to be. You're where I want to be. Everything else is just details."

Her fingers relaxed where they'd

twisted into my shirt, her eyes locked on mine, waiting for me to blink, to backtrack. When I didn't, she exhaled, and the breath that hit my lips felt like heaven.

"You're serious."

"As a drumbeat. I'm not letting us go, Cerys. Not now. Not ever."

She shook her head, a small smile breaking through the tension on her face. "You really think you can juggle all this?"

I grinned, letting my thumb trace a slow line along her jaw. "I'm a drummer. Keeping rhythm is what I do best."

Her laugh escaped before she could stop it, warm and rich, and it hit me square in the chest. God, I'd missed that sound.

"You're an idiot," she said as she pulled me closer.

"And you love me for it." I leaned in until her forehead brushed mine.

"Debatable." Her lips betrayed her, quirking into that maddening smirk that always seemed to challenge me.

I didn't give her time to argue further. My mouth found hers, slow at first, testing, but when her hands tightened in my shirt and her body pressed closer, I let go of every doubt I'd carried for eight years.

I kissed her like a man possessed, like every breath I took was hers to claim. My hands, rough and calloused from years of drumming, slid beneath her shirt, tracing the curves that had haunted my dreams and fuelled my lyrics.

Her pulse fluttered beneath my lips as I pressed soft kisses to her jaw and down the column of her throat, a frantic rhythm that matched the drumbeat of my own heart. Her hot and desperate breath fanned the flames of a desire Id been trying to deny for years. I slid my hands up, taking her shirt with them. She sat up, her eyes locked onto mine, and lifted her arms, letting me strip it off completely.

I paused, taking in the sight of her, the way the firelight danced across her skin, the curve of her waist, the slight tremble of her lips. It cast a warm, golden glow that made her look almost ethereal.

She was gorgeous, not just on the outside, but in a way that spoke to every part of me. There was trust in her eyes, a vulnerability that she was handing to me like a fragile gift. It made me want to be better, to be the kind of man who deserved that trust.

Leaning in, I pressed a gentle kiss to her shoulder and muttered, "You're so fucking beautiful, Cerys."

"I'll never get tired of hearing that," she said, tracing the line of my jaw with her fingertips.

I smiled against her skin, letting my lips linger for a moment before pulling back to meet her gaze. "Good." I brushed a stray strand of hair from her cheek. "Because I don't plan on stopping anytime soon."

Her lips curved into a soft smile, and for a heartbeat, neither of us said anything, the quiet crackle of the fire filling the space. "You've got a lot of time to make up for, Davies."

I laughed. "Oh, I'm counting on it." I captured her hand in mine, pressing a kiss to her palm before guiding it down to the hem of my shirt. She took the hint, pulling it up and over my head, her fingers trailing along my skin and leaving a path of fire in their wake. "And I'll remind you every day if I have to."

Her eyes roamed over my chest. Impatient, I dove for her, a grin splitting my face as I pulled her to my chest and unhooked her bra with a quick flick of my fingers. She laughed, as I tugged her down to the floor, rolling on top of her until she was pinned in the blankets.

"Now, where were we?" I propped myself up on my elbows and gazed down at her.

She flushed while her heart raced against my chest. "You were about to show me just how much you've missed me," she said, her voice rough with desire.

I smiled, brushing a strand of hair away from her face. "That's right." I leaned down, capturing her lips in a slow, deep kiss. She moaned softly, her body arching against mine.

My hands explored her body, tracing the curves I'd barely had a chance to memorise this afternoon. Her breath trembled as my fingers found the waistband of her leggings, teasing the sensitive skin beneath. I broke the kiss, trailing my lips down her neck, her collarbone, until I reached the swell of her breasts.

"Nick," she gasped, her fingers tangling in my hair as I took one nipple into my mouth, swirling my tongue around the sensitive peak.

I hummed in response, the vibration drawing a soft cry from her lips. The sound sent a jolt straight to my cock, making me throb with need.

I moved to her other breast, giving it the same attention, loving how her body responded to my touch. Her fingers threaded through my hair, holding me close. The storm outside rattled the windows, but here, it was just us, lost in our own world of heat and desire.

I trailed my hand down her stomach, her muscles quivered under my touch. Sliding lower again, I cupped her pussy and rubbed her through the material. I wanted to tear the fabric away, to bury myself inside her, but I also wanted to savour this moment, to draw it out and make it last.

Instead, I very deliberately curled my fingers in the waistband and tugged. She lifted her hips, helping me, and I slid both her leggings and underwear down her thighs, her calves, her ankles, until she was bare before me.

The fire crackled in the hearth, casting flickering shadows on Cerys's skin as I ran my hands up her legs, a slow journey from her ankles to her thighs. Her breath hitched as I brushed against her soaking pussy. I pressed a soft kiss to her inner thigh, and she squirmed, her hips lifting as if to urge me on.

"If you don't put your mouth on me right now, I'll make you eat your own drumsticks."

I laughed, low and deep, letting her words linger as I kissed up her thigh, getting closer and closer to where she wanted me, but never quite there. "Bold threat, Evans. I'd love to see you try, but I'm a bit busy right now."

"Busy stalling," she snapped, her voice sharp but breathless. "You'd think eight years of touring would've taught you some bloody efficiency."

"Is that what you want for our first time as a couple?" I glanced up, raising a brow as I pressed another kiss to her mound, just above her glistening lips. "Quick and forgettable? I thought you'd appreciate a bit more finesse."

She groaned, her head falling back against the cushions. "What I want is for you to stop proving you can talk in circles and actually do something."

"Do something?" My voice dipped lower as I nipped at her skin, earning a moan. "You make it sound like I haven't already spent half the day showing you exactly how I feel."

"Half the day isn't enough." Her fingers curled into my hair and tugged just enough to make her point clear. "You're a drummer, Nick. Aren't you supposed to have better timing?"

I shook my head as I kissed her other thigh, closer to where I knew she wanted me. "Fine. You win. But don't say I didn't warn you when I make this a moment you'll replay on a loop."

She laughed, the sound tinged with a challenge. "Then stop talking and prove it, rock star."

And I did. Over and over, until her

breathless laughter turned into quiet whispers, and the storm outside faded into the background. It wasn't perfect, and it didn't erase the years we'd lost — but it was ours. Messy and complicated, like everything about us had always been. But for the first time, it felt like we weren't chasing or running. We were exactly where we belonged.

NICK

"Stop eating the batter," Cerys said, swatting at my hand with a wooden spoon. "You've already had half of it."

I licked the edge of my finger, grinning as she glared at me. "Tastes better raw."

"You're worse than a toddler," Cerys said, snatching the whisk out of my hand. "Honestly, do you need a snack to tide you over?"

I grinned, leaning my hip against the counter. "Depends. Are you offering?"

She rolled her eyes, brushing her braid over her shoulder as she turned back to the bowl. "You're going to get in the way if you don't find something useful to do."

I leaned in close, resting my chin on her shoulder. "I am being useful. Moral support is a vital part of pancake-making."

She arched an eyebrow, her hands pausing over the bowl. "You've done nothing but sabotage me since we started."

"Sabotage is a strong word." I reached for the wooden spoon she'd set down, twirling it between my fingers. "Let's call it... creative input."

Her laugh was a soft huff as she nudged me with her elbow, a warm press against my ribs that made me wish I could stay exactly like this forever. "If you're so full of creative input, why don't you take over?"

"Because," I said, giving her braid a gentle tug as I straightened up, "watching you is far more fun."

Her lips twitched, but she didn't look up. "You say that like you're getting away with something."

I leaned against the counter, spinning the wooden spoon like a drumstick. "Maybe I am."

"Careful, Nick. I've got flour and I'm not afraid to use it."

"I'd like to see you try."

She glanced at me then, the challenge sparking in her eyes. "You're all talk."

I straightened, setting the spoon down with deliberate care. "You sure about that?"

"Positive."

The batter hit me square in the chest before I even saw her move. Warm, sticky, and sweet-smelling, it dripped down my jumper in slow, mocking trails. I stared at her, mouth open in shock.

"You didn't."

She raised the whisk, the corner of her mouth quirking. "Want to test me again?"

I took a slow step forward, swiping the batter from my chest and holding it up. "That was a mistake, Evans."

She laughed, backing up as I advanced. "Nick! Don't you dare."

Her warning only made me grin wider. "You started this."

I lunged, catching her wrist before she could retaliate with the whisk. She yelped, laughing as I pulled her closer, the batter on my hand now streaked across her apron.

"Nick!" she shrieked, squirming against my hold, but I was laughing too hard to let go. "Payback," I said, smearing another streak of batter on her arm.

She gasped, a scandalised sound that melted into laughter as she wrested her wrist free. "You absolute menace! Do you even know how hard it is to scrub dried batter out of fabric?"

I grinned, already reaching for another glob. "Guess you'll have to be quicker next time."

Her eyes narrowed, her mouth curving into a dangerous smile. "Oh, you want quick?"

Before I could react, she ducked under my arm, grabbing a handful of batter from the bowl. I barely had time to step back before she smeared it across my cheek, her triumphant laugh echoing off the kitchen walls.

"Now you've done it," I said, wiping at my face as she darted out of reach.

She held her ground, her chin lifted in challenge. "Bring it on, rock star."

"Oh, I will." I lunged, but she was already moving, darting around the table with a laugh that made my chest ache in the best way. She grabbed the mixing bowl as she passed, holding it like a shield.

"Stay back," she said, her voice firm with a warning edge, though the curve of her lips betrayed her. "Or the batter gets it."

"You're bluffing," I said, circling the table slowly. "You wouldn't sacrifice breakfast."

"Wouldn't I?" She tipped the bowl slightly, letting a thin ribbon of batter drip onto the table.

"Cerys!" I stopped, my hands raised in surrender. "Alright, alright. No more batter wars."

She tilted her head, eyeing me suspiciously. "Promise?"

"Promise." I stepped closer, keeping my movements slow. "Truce?"

Her grip on the bowl relaxed, her shoulders easing. "Truce."

The second she set the bowl down, I made my move, swooping in to grab her around the waist. She shrieked, half-laughing, half-protesting as I hoisted her off the ground and spun us both in a tight circle.

"Nick!" she yelled, her fists lightly thudding against my shoulders. "Put me down!"

"Say I win." I held her just high enough that her feet dangled.

"You're lucky I'm not holding the whisk," she shouted, but there was no heat in her voice, just laughter that she couldn't contain.

"That's not an answer," I said, slowing my spin but keeping her firmly in my hold.

Her hands gripped my shoulders, her cheeks flushed and her chest heaving. "Alright! You win. Now put me down."

I lowered her to the floor, keeping her close even as she swatted at me. Her eyes sparkled, her lips parted in a smile she didn't bother to hide.

"Happy now?" she asked, her voice softening as she met my gaze.

"Getting there."

I leaned in, capturing her lips with mine, a gentle brush that quickly ignited into something deeper. Her breath snagged, and I savoured the moment, the warmth and softness of her mouth an intoxicating mix. Each touch, each kiss sent a surge of electricity through me, filling my heart with something I'd only ever found with her. Her hands gripped my shirt, pulling me closer. I deepened the kiss, my tongue tracing her lips, coaxing them open, revelling in the simple fact that I could kiss her like this — whenever I wanted — now that she was mine.

"I knew it," she said, her voice filled with satisfaction. "Took you long enough."

We jolted apart at the sound of Meinir's voice, her tone brimming with unrestrained glee. My hands dropped to my sides while Cerys fumbled to smooth her hair, her cheeks flushed.

Meinir stood in the doorway, arms crossed, a wide grin lighting her face. Her boots tracked faint smudges of mud onto the floor, but she didn't seem to notice. Her sharp eyes darted between us, and she let out a soft laugh, warm and knowing.

Cerys groaned, brushing a hand over her braid. "Meins, please."

"What?" Meinir's grin widened. "I'm just saying, it's about time. Gareth would've had a good laugh about how long it's taken you two to figure this out."

Her words tightened something in my chest, but I didn't let it take root. For years, I'd let Gareth's memory hold me back, like every step towards Cerys was a betrayal. I'd blinded myself to the truth — what we had wasn't about Gareth at all.

"I think he'd want this for us," I said, my voice firm. I glanced at Cerys, finding her green eyes steady on mine. "And I want this. I want you."

Her lips parted, something soft and surprised flickering across her face before she squeezed my hand.

Meinir watched us, her smile warm now, her eyes glistening with emotion. "You're right," she said, her voice quieter but still strong. "He'd want you both to be happy."

I nodded, my jaw tightening as I let go of the last hesitation I'd clung to for years. "I've been holding myself back for too long," I admitted, glancing down at our joined hands. "But not anymore. Cerys, I—" I broke off, clearing my throat. "I'll do whatever it takes to make this work. I want you more than anything."

Cerys's hand tightened in mine, her smile breaking into something that made my chest ache in the best way. "You're already doing it," she said softly.

Meinir clapped her hands, cutting through the moment with a laugh that carried no small amount of triumph. "Finally! Well, it's official, then. You two are together. Don't even try to deny it."

Cerys pinched the bridge of her nose, her other hand still locked in mine. "If I say yes, will you stop looking like you've won the lottery?"

"Not a chance," Meinir said, leaning against the counter. "This is better than the lottery. I've been waiting years for you two to stop being idiots."

I chuckled, glancing at Cerys, who groaned softly but didn't pull her hand away. "Alright, Meins, you win. You were right. And... thank you."

Meinir's smile softened, her gaze flicking between us with a mix of pride and affection. "Don't thank me yet. You've still got to clean my kitchen."

Cerys muttered something under her breath, and I couldn't resist pulling her closer, tilting my head to catch her eye. "What was that?"

She sighed, though there was a spark of humour in her eyes. "I said she's never going to let us live this down."

"Too right," Meinir said, already moving towards the table to inspect the damage. "But don't worry — I'll only remind you every time I see you."

I turned to Cerys, brushing a stray bit of flour from her cheek. "Reckon we'll survive?"

She smiled up at me, small but genuine. "As long as you're willing to scrub every pan, maybe."

Meinir barked a laugh from across the room. "You two had better get started. That batter's not going to clean itself."

Cerys reached for the cloth, but I caught her wrist, tugging her back towards me.

"Not yet," I murmured, my voice low enough that only she could hear. "I need to kiss you again first."

"Meins is right there," she hissed, her

eyes darting towards where Meinir was rummaging in a cupboard, clearly pretending not to eavesdrop.

"So?" I said, lowering my voice and leaning closer. "She's already planning a parade. Might as well give her something to celebrate."

Cerys's lips parted, her cheeks still flushed. "You're shameless."

"And you love it," I said, closing the space between us without waiting for a reply.

Her breath faltered, but she didn't pull away. I caught her lips with mine, soft at first, savouring the moment, then deeper, more certain. Her hand slid up to my chest, her grip tightening as if she wasn't planning to let go anytime soon.

Behind us, Meinir let out an exaggerated cough.

"Do I need to get the hose?" she said, her voice full of laughter and absolutely no shame.

Cerys broke away, spinning to face her, her face redder than the batter-streaked counter. "Meins!"

"What?" Meinir said, grinning so wide

she practically glowed. "I've waited long enough for this moment. You're not going to stop me from enjoying it."

I laughed, still holding Cerys's hand as she muttered something under her breath, avoiding Meinir's gleeful gaze.

"Fine," Cerys finally said, her voice quieter but steady. "You were right, okay? Is that what you wanted to hear?"

Meinir placed a hand over her heart, her expression falsely solemn. "More than you know."

I glanced at Cerys. "She deserves it," I said, my voice low. "After all, she did get us here."

Cerys sighed, shaking her head but smiling as she squeezed my hand. "Thank you, Meins. For meddling."

Meinir clapped her hands, practically bouncing on her feet. "You're welcome. Now, get on with breakfast before I faint from hunger. And don't think I'm not telling everyone I know."

Cerys groaned, burying her face in her hands, but I just laughed, leaning down to kiss her temple. "Let her have this," I whispered. "She's earned it."

Her hand lowered, her smile softening as she looked up at me. "You might regret saying that when she starts planning our wedding."

"I'll risk it," I said, kissing her again before grabbing the sponge to tackle the mess.

*W*ant more Nick and Cerys?

Their story doesn't end here. Discover what happens when Nick, miles away on the road, gifts Cerys a *very personal* device—and takes control, no matter the distance.

I usually reserve this for my mailing list but this is easier in print. Plus, it's just nice to have it all together, right?

Turn the page to read.

If you enjoyed *Rockstar Regret* please consider leaving a review on your preferred platform.

Six weeks later

CERYS

"Fancy a midnight striptease for your biggest fan?" Nick's voice sounded from my phone, warm and husky. An invitation that made my pulse kick up a gear.

I sat on the floor of my bedroom wrapped in a towel, trying to use the laundry as a distraction from the stress over tomorrow's cheese competition. One smile from him, and it all faded.

He lounged on a hotel bed in Madrid. It had been four weeks since Nick left for Europe to support The Brightside. Every night he called me, tired but buzzing with excitement for the next stop. Even now, hours after his set, hints of stage adrenaline still clung to him.

"Caught you at a thrilling time, I see." He motioned to the pile of socks perched on the bed behind me.

I tightened my towel. "I'll have you know my day has been pure excitement — eight hours of cheese prep, a phone call with a marketing rep, and an epic battle with my washing basket. Still want that striptease?"

He rubbed his jaw, an amused spark lighting his expression. "You could throw on a robe. Unless you want an audience." His soft laugh drifted through the speaker. "Though I'm not complaining about the view."

Despite the miles, these moments made it feel like he was right here with me.

He'd made good on his promise, moving in with me over Christmas. For two glorious weeks, I got him all to myself. He was a hurricane of teasing affection, constantly pulling me back into bed, leaving it a tangled mess more often than not.

"Stop flirting." My cheeks burned. "Big day on this end, remember?"

"I don't know why you're stressing." He lay down with a devil-may-care grin that could melt a glacier. "You're going to wipe the floor with the lot of them. Your cheeses are the best in Wales, and everyone knows it."

Despite his confidence, a ripple of anxiety tightened my chest. "Easy for you to say, rock star. You're not the one facing a panel of judges with a palate more refined than a sommelier on steroids."

Nick chuckled, the sound low and reassuring. "If they've got half a brain, they'll see what I do. And if they don't, well, maybe they just have terrible taste."

I snorted, tossing a sock onto the growing pile. "Right. Blame the judges. That'll look great on the feedback forms."

He stretched lazily, his arm flopping off the edge of the bed like he had all the time in the world. "I'm serious. If they can't appreciate brilliance, then the problem's theirs. You're bloody brilliant, babe. End of."

I rolled my eyes, though the warmth in

his voice tugged at something deep in my chest. "Well, thanks for the glowing review, Professor Cheese."

"I can't wait to see your face when you win. You'll call me once you know, right?"

"Of course." My heart stuttered at his certainty. "Wish you could be here. Or I could be in Madrid." A pang of longing twisted inside me, but I masked it with a soft grin. He raked a hand through his hair, a lazy grin spreading across his face. "The energy was mad tonight. Felt like they were just as hyped for Lover's Knot as they were for The Brightside. Could've sworn I saw a bloke in the front row with our logo tattooed on his arm."

"Bet you were tempted to autograph it."

"Nah, I'm saving my penmanship for your competition trophy," he said, bringing the phone closer to his face, his grin softening into something quieter. "But seriously, it wasn't the same. Hard to enjoy it when my favourite person's on the other side of the channel."

"I miss you too," I said, the words slipping out as easy as breathing. "I can't wait for Rome. Three weeks feels like forever."

"You've got no idea how much I'm looking forward to that. Just you, me, and a proper espresso that doesn't taste like jet fuel."

I laughed, the sound breaking the tension that had crept up on me. "And you call me high maintenance."

He tilted his head, mock-serious. "I think I've earned it, don't you? Surviving weeks of hotel coffee is no small feat."

I rolled my eyes. "All right, martyr. When I see you, I'll buy you the biggest cappuccino Rome has to offer."

He smirked. "Speaking of surprises... did you check under the stairs?"

My eyes narrowed. "Why? What have you done now?"

"Nothing sinister," he said, his grin shifting into something far too innocent to be trusted. "Just... go have a look."

I gave him a pointed look but stood anyway, the phone in my hand as I walked down the stairs and into the hallway. Flicking on the light, I peered into the cupboard.

"Where am I looking?" I asked, nudging aside a shoebox that had somehow ended up in the cupboard. I kept my house fairly tidy, but this cupboard always seemed to attract stray odds and ends.

"Behind the baubles," Nick said, his tone carrying that infuriating blend of smugness and charm. "Unless you've gone on a cleaning spree since I left."

"Har har." I nudged the box aside.

I'd been busy, okay? Who cared if the under-stair cupboard overflowed?

I snatched up a brown-paper-covered box and shuffled back into the light.

"Do not open until I say so," I read aloud, holding the box up for him to see. His handwriting scrawled across the paper looked as casual as the smirk plastered on his face. "Should I be worried?"

"Not at all." Nick shuffled up the bed and leaned back against the headboard like he hadn't a care in the world. "Although, I'd prepare for something life changing."

I snorted, walking back up the stairs. "Last time you said that I ended up with a pair of socks that played Jingle Bells when I walked."

"And you wore them for a whole week." His grin only widened. "Now quit stalling."

I shook my head at the idiot, unable to keep the smile from claiming my lips. I plopped the package onto the bed and tore at the paper. Beneath it was a sleek, glossy black box, minimalist in design except for the unmistakable brand name printed across the top in gold letters. One I'd definitely heard of before, thanks to late-night podcasts and nosy friends.

My smile froze.

"Nick," I said slowly. "Why does this look like... what I think it is?"

His grin stretched wider, utterly unapologetic. "What does it look like?"

I popped the lid off the box and was greeted by a sleek, compact device nestled in velvet. The elegant, modern design only made it worse.

"Oh my God." I held it up between two fingers like it might bite me. "Nick. You did not."

"I absolutely did," he said, revelling in

my reaction. "State of the art. Fully app-controlled."

"App-controlled?" I spluttered, glancing between the vibrator and the screen. "How — why — what on earth possessed you to think this was a good idea?"

"Jared recommended it. Said it's great for couples dealing with, you know, a bit of distance."

My jaw dropped. "Jared recommended this?"

"Yup, and Ella backed him up. Said it was a game-changer."

If someone had told me all those years ago that we'd end up here, I wouldn't have believed them — but now, I couldn't imagine being with anyone else. Could the man be any more adorable?

"And honestly, it's practical. Thoughtful, even," Nick said, unrepentant as ever.

"Thoughtful?" I held the thing closer to the camera like he hadn't fully grasped what he'd left me. "Nick, you left me a vibrator."

"A top-of-the-range vibrator." His grin

was downright devilish now. "Customisable settings, whisper-quiet motor…"

Before he could finish his sales pitch, the thing buzzed to life in my hand. I let out a yelp and dropped it onto the bed, my heart thudding in my chest. "Nick!"

His laughter exploded through the call, unrestrained. "You should've seen your face! Priceless."

"Turn it off!" I demanded, jabbing at the buttons, but the device seemed determined to defy me, vibrating in a maddening rhythm. "Nick, I swear—"

"I've got it." His brow furrowed as he tapped on the screen. The buzzing stopped abruptly, leaving only the sound of his laughter echoing through the call.

I glared at the screen, though the corners of my mouth betrayed me, twitching upward despite myself. "You're an absolute menace."

"And you're adorable when you're flustered," he said, his grin softening just enough to let something warmer shine through. "Admit it — you're impressed."

I grabbed the box and shoved the vibrator back inside. "Three weeks. Three weeks until I see you in Rome. You'd better pray I've cooled off by then."

"You'll miss me before then," he said confidently, leaning back against the pillows like the king of everything.

I sighed, unable to fight the laugh bubbling out of me. "Miss you already, idiot."

His smile softened, his voice dipping lower. "Miss you too. Every bloody day."

I stared at the device again, my cheeks burning. Bloody hell, this thing wasn't messing around.

It wasn't just any vibrator; it was an elaborate contraption designed to tease and tantalise in ways that made my heart pound and my breath catch.

It had a hood that promised to give my clit some serious attention, but that wasn't the part making my pulse race. Nor was it due to the dildo that would fill my pussy.

That honour went to the smaller extension that would press against my ass, promising a whole new level of sensation.

"What's that look for?" Nick asked, his smirk almost audible. The sod knew exactly what thoughts were squirrelling away inside my head.

"This thing is intense."

And I knew he was serious before, but this... this felt like him going out of his way to make sure we worked, no matter the distance.

"Intense can be good." His voice dropped even lower. "Why don't we take it for a test drive?"

I shook my head. "No way. I can't just—"

"It's no different than every night since I left. Only this time, I get to take a little more control."

"Is that so?" I raised a brow. "And what makes you think I'll just hand over the reins?"

Nick's grin was slow and sexy, making my heart do a little flip. "Because, Cerys," he said, drawing out my name in a way that made my toes curl, "you know you want to. You're curious. I can see it in your eyes."

I snorted, but my cheeks heated. Bloody hell, he was right. I was curious.

I bit my lip, glancing between the box and his expectant face. "Fine." I sighed. "But only because I'm curious."

"That's the spirit." He shifted up his bed, propping himself up against the headboard. "Now, let's get you set up."

I hesitated, suddenly feeling a bit self-conscious. "Set up how, exactly?"

His eyes gleamed with desire. "Prop your phone up somewhere I can see you."

I hesitated, my heart pounding in my chest. But the look in his eyes, even through the screen, was enough to make me give in. I propped my phone up against a pile of pillows on his side of the bed, making sure he had a clear view of me.

"Now lose the towel."

I rolled my eyes but complied, letting the damp towel drop to the floor. The cool air of my bedroom hit my skin, making me shiver. Or maybe it was the way Nick's gaze roved over me, hungry and appreciative.

"God, you're gorgeous," he murmured, his voice thick with desire. "Now, grab the toy and get comfortable."

I picked up the vibrator. It was sleek and smooth, the silicone soft against my fingertips. I climbed onto the bed, my breath hitching as our eyes caught through the screen, and lay down.

"Good," he said, his voice low and commanding. "Are you wet?"

I hesitated, the burn in my cheeks creeping down my neck. I shuffled around on the bed, unsure of how to arrange myself.

"Stop fidgeting, Cerys," Nick said, his voice low and teasing. "It's just me. You're safe."

I bit my lip, trying to hide the nervous excitement that bubbled inside me. This was new, but not entirely unfamiliar. Four weeks of nightly calls had led to this moment. "I know. I'm not nervous. Just... getting comfortable."

"Right." He chuckled, the sound warm and intimate. "Christ, look at you. Already blushing before we've even started."

I crossed my arms over my chest, skin pebbling under his gaze. "Some of us are more modest than rock stars."

"Clearly I need to work harder to free you of those pesky inhibitions." He smirked, leaning back and stretching, his muscles shifting under the fabric. "We've got three weeks before I'm fucking you in a storage cupboard backstage."

My eyes widened. Why did the idea of it both terrify and thrill me?

"What makes you think I'd be into that?"

Nick's grin only widened. "Because, Cerys my love, you've got that look in your eyes. The one that says you're already imagining it." His voice dropped lower, a husky rumble that sent shivers down my spine. "Touch yourself. Tell me how wet you are."

I hesitated, feeling a mix of excitement and nerves. But the look in his eyes, that hungry, intense gaze, spurred me on. I reached down, sliding my fingers between my thighs. I was already slick, the evidence of my arousal coating my fingers.

"I could just lie to you."

"And I'd know. You're not that good of a liar, Cerys." His grin was slow and sexy, even through the screen. "Now, tell me."

My throat tightened, but I forced a scoff. "Bossy tonight, aren't we?"

"Always." His gaze sharpened, stripping me bare. "But you like it."

I did. God help me, I did.

I swallowed, the heat in my cheeks spreading. "I'm wet."

"Show me." His gaze locked onto mine, not letting me look away.

I hesitated, biting my lip. Then, slowly, I brought my fingers up to the camera, giving him a clear view. His eyes darkened, the look in them sending a thrill through me.

"Good," Nick said, his voice a low growl. "Now touch yourself until you're on the edge."

I pressed two fingers against my clit, circling once. Fire licked up my spine. "Fuck."

"Tell me how it feels."

I dragged my fingers lower, slickness coating them. "It feels good, but it's not enough."

A groan tore from him, hand sliding beneath the waistband of his joggers. "Christ. Keep going."

I plunged two fingers inside, back arching at the stretch. "N-Nick—"

"Fuck, yes. Just like that." His fist

moved in his lap, pace matching mine. "Are you ready for more?"

My hips rolled, driving my fingers harder. "Y-yes."

"Wish I was pounding into you until you scream." The raw hunger in his voice unravelled me. "But the vibrator is just going to have to stand in."

Heat pooled lower. "Arrogant prick."

"Your arrogant prick." His grin turned feral. "Now grab the toy. Tease your pretty pussy with it."

I pulled the vibrator back out of the box and gripped it tight, the silicone warming under my palm. I stared at the ridged thing for a second, amused at how much it looked like some ridiculous alien artefact. Then I lowered it between my legs and did as Nick told me.

"Start slow. Glide it through your folds — yeah, just like that."

The silicone tip caught my clit, wringing a whimper from my throat. "Ohgod—"

"There she is." Pride laced his words. "Now press it inside. Little by little."

I guided the toy to my entrance, pressure building as the tip breached me. "T-too much—"

"Breathe, babe." His voice softened, thumb stroking the screen like he could touch me. "You're taking it so well. Just a bit more…"

The stretch burned deliciously, my walls fluttering around the intrusion. "Nick, I—!"

"Shh, I've got you." His rasp gentled, coaxing. "Now move it. Slow. Feel every ridge."

I dragged the toy out, then back in, moaning at the drag. "S'different. Not as good as your cock, but good."

He stilled, jaw clenching. "Fuck, Cerys—"

The admission spilled out, reckless. "Miss how you stretch me."

A growl vibrated through the speaker.

Without warning, the device powered up, and the first buzz hit like lightning. My back arched off the mattress, a gasp tearing from my throat as the dildo vibrated, the clit suction attached and the anal probe did something I couldn't even name. Nick's low laugh crackled through the speaker.

"That's one," he said, voice rough as gravel. "Twenty-seven more and I break my high score."

I fumbled for the phone, nearly knocking it off the pillows. "You're keeping count?"

"Every time you come undone? Absolutely." His smirk blurred through the screen. "Now spread your legs wider. Want to watch you take it all."

The tri-pressure drove coherence from my brain. My hips jerked, chasing the rhythm he controlled from another country.

"Nick—"

"Tell me."

"Feels like you're here." I dug my heels into the sheets, the stretch bordering on too much. "Like you're fucking me—"

A sharp inhale from his end. The pattern shifted, waves cresting then retreating. Torture.

"Missed this," he growled. "Missed *you.* That tight little gasp you make right before—"

The orgasm ripped through me without warning. White static filled my vision, muscles clamping around nothing.

"Christ, Cerys." Nick's curse cut through the haze. "The sounds you make. Better than any music."

I lay boneless, watching condensation drip down the windowpane. The device still hummed, gentler now.

"You okay?"

I blinked at his softened tone. No teasing, just... Nick.

"Still here." My voice came out raspy. "Just... didn't expect it to work that well."

Silence. Then—

"I'm coming home."

I froze. "Your tour—"

"Fuck the tour. Pryderi can dock my pay." Sheets rustled as he shifted. "Shouldn't have left."

"Don't." I sat up, clutching the phone. "You've waited years for this break. I'm not your damsel."

"You're my *everything*." The raw ache in his words stole my breath. "Hate that I can't— That I'm not—" I traced his pixelated jawline, throat tight.

"Three weeks," I whispered.

"Eighteen days."

"Then you can wreck me properly in Rome."

His laugh shook. "Gonna make you scream so loud they hear you in Vatican City."

I fell back onto the pillows, spent and smiling.

Three weeks felt like forever, but after eight years apart, what was a little more waiting? We'd already faced the heartbreak, the silence, and all the mistakes we couldn't take back. The miles didn't matter — not when we'd finally found our way back to each other. It wouldn't be easy, but nothing worth keeping ever was. We had this.Because this time, we weren't letting go.

Thank you for reading Rockstar Regret. I hope you enjoyed it.

ALSO BY MORGANA BEVAN

True Platinum Series (Rock Star Romance)

(Rhiannon)

Chasing Alys–Ryan (Resistant to Love)

Charming Daphne–Matt (Force Proximity)

Winning Nia–James (Second Chance)

Enticing Mel–Dan (Secret Baby)

Needing Emily–Emily (Accidental Marriage/Runaway Bride)

Defying Ella - Jared (Close Proximity / Snowed-in)

(The Brightside)

Braving Lily - Lily (Opposites Attract)

Daring Ceri - Alex (Second Chance)

Marrying Olivia - Lewis (Accidental Marriage)

Craving Leah - Andy (Best Friend's Sister)

Lovers Knot

Rockstar Regret - Nick (Forced Proximity)

Kings of Screen Series (Hollywood Romance)

Between Takes (Enemies to Lovers)

Married Blind (Marriage of Convenience)

Acting Counsel (Close Proximity, Forbidden)

Fashionably Fake (Fake Dating)

Lights, Camera, Baby! (Accidental Pregnancy)

<u>Written as Selina Bevan</u>

Standalones

Infernal Bargain (MF Witch Romance)

The Morrigan Soul Bond Series

Bound By The Goddess (Why Choose Witch Romance)

Marked By The Goddess (Why Choose Witch Romance)

Morgana Bevan is a sucker for a rock star romance, particularly if it involves a soul-destroying breakup or strangers waking up in Vegas. She's a contemporary romance author based in Wales. When Morgana's not writing steamy rock star and movie star romances, she's working in TV production in the UK.

She enjoys travelling, attending gigs, and trying out the extreme activities she forces on her characters.

Find Morgana online at morganabevan.com.

www.ingramcontent.com/pod-product-compliance
Lightning Source LLC
Chambersburg PA
CBHW032000180726
48283CB00008B/2514